Monday 3rd September

Hello blog! It's the start of another term and there are three things that SUCK about my life:

1. I am STILL sharing a bedroom with my step-brother Gav (AKA Shrek's stinkier twin).
2. My mum is 6 months pregnant and therefore cabbage-kickingly MENTAL.
3. I'm about to have a high speed rail line (i.e. brace) installed in my gob!

The only non-sucky thing is that I've got a GIRLFRIEND! A real one! Who actually wants to SNOG me!!! The problem is there's this smarmy tossbag called Seb trying to steal her off me with his rubbish DJ skills.

There's just one thing for it—me and my best mates Harry and Ad are going to enter the same DJ competition as Seb and WIN!

What could POSSIBLY go wrong?

Dedicated to everyone who was traumatised by the end of the last book.

OXFORD
UNIVERSITY PRESS

Great Clarendon Street, Oxford OX2 6DP
Oxford University Press is a department of the University of Oxford.
It furthers the University's objective of excellence in research, scholarship,
and education by publishing worldwide in

Oxford New York

Oxford is a registered trademark of Oxford University Press
in the UK and in certain other countries

Text Copyright © Ben Davis 2016
Illustrations Copyright © Mike Lowery 2016

The moral rights of the author and illustrator have been asserted

Database right Oxford University Press (maker)

First published 2016

British Library Cataloguing in Publication Data

Data available

ISBN: 978-0-19-274481-4

1 3 5 7 9 10 8 6 4 2

Printed in Great Britain
Paper used in the production of this book is a natural,
recyclable product made from wood grown in sustainable forests.
The manufacturing process conforms to the environmental
regulations of the country of origin.

All images from Shutterstock and OUP

THE PRIVATE BLOG OF

JOE COWLEY

WELCOME TO

CRINGEFEST

WRITTEN BY
BEN DAVIS

OXFORD
UNIVERSITY PRESS

Sunday 23rd June

Right, blog. I'm back.

Let's not waste time with pleasantries.

Top ten reasons why everything is terrible

• The love of my life, Natalie, still hates me just because I made one tiny mistake. OK, we had a row and I kissed my ex, so it was kind of a huge mistake. I am so distraught about this that I can't even muster the energy to smile or go for a haircut. I look like a depressed Wookiee.

• Due to my depressed state, my academic career is suffering. I've been preparing for my GCSEs for the past five years like they're the most important things in the world but now they seem so pointless. I mean, what good are qualifications going to do me when I'm a hermit, living in a cave somewhere, drinking my own tears?

• Despite all that, I do still want to go to college. Mainly because Natalie is going there with my so-called 'friend' Greeny. You see, recently they've started hanging out together a lot—before school, during school, after school. ALL THE COCKING TIME. And to top it off, I've just found out that I can't get into college to put a stop to this madness because my predicted grades aren't good enough. 'Predicted grades?' Give me a break. They didn't destroy the Borg Queen for 'predicted' forcible assimilation of other sentient species, did they?

• Natalie and Greeny being close friends wouldn't have bothered me before, but since January, Greeny has lost like, half of his body weight, and now girls actually fancy him. But guess what? He's not interested in other girls, only Natalie. Isn't that WONDERFUL?

• My twin sisters, Holly and Ivy, have barely stopped crying since they were born. This means most of my nights are spent lying in the dark listening to a sickening mixture of babies screaming and my stepbrother Gav in the bunk above my head, farting and scratching his crotch. Plus, they've been given the spare room that became available when Gav's nan, Doris, moved out. Um, hello? I've been here for sixteen years, and they only popped out five minutes ago. If this were Coasterville, they'd have been ejected for queue-jumping.

• Not only do I still have braces, I now also have to have this horrible metal retainer strapped to my face at night, which makes me look like the crappest cyborg you've ever seen in your life.

• Mum and Jim have decided that they're getting married on the 10th of August. This means that very soon I will have to spend a day with my ridiculous extended family, including Uncle Johnny and his creepy-as-hell collection of ventriloquist dummies.

• Gav has got a job in a warehouse so he's hardly ever at home. To begin with, I thought this would be a good thing, but it just means I have nothing to distract me from my crushing, debilitating misery.

• After their runner-up placing in the Bangaz Radio DJ competition, Harry, Ad, and (damn him to hell) Greeny aka the *SOUND EXPERIENCE* have gained a bigger fan base, especially in the gay community. All because I came up with the gimmick of Harry and Ad pretending to be a couple. How did they capitalize on this? By releasing a remix of 'YMCA'? A cover of 'Somewhere Over the Rainbow'? No, they sampled me saying 'I'm as gay as the day is long,' on the radio and turned it into a club hit. It made the top ten in the dance charts.

• There's a school yearbook because we're leaving. We had to have our photos taken and come up with a quote. I was too depressed to bother, so the committee did one for me. I probably should have seen it coming.

I'M AS GAY AS THE DAY IS LONG

Monday 24th June

Why haven't you killed me yet?

We had to be in our form room this afternoon for a last minute revision lesson. Mr Shenko was late so we were all lounging around doing nothing.

I sat at my desk, staring at my precious stuffed zombie toy. Natalie bought it me for our three month anniversary. She said it was to symbolize that she would love me even after she died and came back as a brain-hungry member of the undead. It was proper romantic.

As I stared into its green, decomposing face, my thoughts, as they often do, returned to that night at the DJ competition final. Me seeing old photos of Natalie and that smarmy moron Seb together. Storming off and ending up at the fountain in Trafalgar Square. Lisa arriving. Giving her my coat. Lisa kissing me. Me not stopping it. Natalie seeing the whole thing. Lying on the floor after being punched in the stomach.

While this recurring nightmare boomeranged around my brain for the fifty-squillionth time, Harry was berating me about how I needed to get over her and move on with my life and blah, blah, blah, I wasn't really listening. In the end, he got so hacked off that he grabbed the zombie and threw it out of the window.

I jumped from my chair, screamed and ran to the scene of the atrocity. The zombie had rolled along the flat roof into the gutter. I grabbed Harry by the lapels of his blazer.

'What the cocking hell did you do that for?' I yelled.

'I'm helping you, old bean,' he said. 'You need to let go of the past. And you can start by letting go of the zombie.'

I shook him hard. 'But I sleep with that!'

'Ugh, and you touched it with your hands, Harry!' said Ad.

'Not like that, you moron,' I said. 'I'm going to have to get it back now.'

I jumped up onto the table.

'Oh my God, Puke's gone mental!' Craig Jackaman shouted.

Puke? Honestly, you throw up over ONE person behind the waltzer and you're marked for life.

Everyone in the class cheered as I hoisted myself up. Harry grabbed my legs but I kicked him off. He had done enough damage. I had to get the zombie back.

The window was only just wide enough for me to squeeze through but I managed it. Well, almost. My feet were stuck and I was hanging upside down, looking back into the classroom. Everyone banged on the glass and cheered me on. I kicked the air and wriggled out of my shoes, before landing shoulder first on the roof with a thud.

I held my throbbing arm and cursed Harry's name to Lord Satan himself. Of all the stupid things he has done over the years, this had to be number one. And I'm talking about someone who once started his own 'free-range ant farm'.

I sprinted over to the edge of the roof where the zombie lay. I picked it up and examined it, trying to ignore the shouts from behind me. It was completely covered in mucky gutter crap. I was trying to wipe the worst of the grime off when a shout from below stopped me.

'Joe!'

I looked down and there was the head teacher, Mr Pratt. He was probably on the way back from his daily cigarette confiscation walk. He had yoinked dozens off Gav over the years.

'Listen, I know you've been depressed lately, but please don't do it!'

DON'T DO IT!

I glanced down at the zombie, then back at him. 'Do what?'

'Jump!' he said.

I looked back at the window. By this time, Mr Shenko had arrived. It was only then that I realized what this must have looked like. I mean, I wasn't high enough to kill myself anyway. Maybe a broken leg but that was about it. Still, Pratt wasn't going to risk it.

'What's going on here?'

Oh, cocking marvellous. Mr Boocock, evil nemesis and sadistic PE teacher, wandered out of the sports equipment container. He looked up at me.

'Please, Joe,' said Pratt. 'I know things seem bleak now, but they won't always. We all value you as a human being!'

'Do we?' said Boocock.

Pratt tutted. 'Please, Mr Boocock, go and find me a ladder. Time is of the essence!'

Boocock folded his arms. 'No can do. Not insured to handle them.' He glanced up at me and gave me a sly smirk. It's like he hates me. Just because I (accidentally) caused him to break his ribs and (accidentally) hoofed him in the spud sack with a massive football boot. Some people just don't know how to let go.

'Can't you see this is an emergency?' said Pratt.

'Best I can do is a crashmat,' Boocock replied.

'Fine.' Pratt rubbed his forehead as Boocock disappeared into the equipment container and reappeared with a big blue mat. It was quite fun watching this all unfold in a way.

'Everything is OK, Joe,' said Pratt in a shaky voice. 'Just stay where you are.'

He spotted the old caretaker, Mr Groggit, shuffling past and called him over.

'A ladder?' said Groggit. He squinted up at me through his thicker-than-aeroplane-windows glasses and scratched his bald head. 'I haven't got one big enough. I asked for one but you said the school couldn't afford it.'

'Yeah, so this is your fault, Pratt,' said Boocock.

'Welcome to the twenty-first century,' said Mr Pratt. 'I couldn't sign off on a ladder because I had to put a new roof on the chemistry lab.'

This was getting embarrassing. 'Look,' I said. 'I can just climb back in through the window if you want?'

Pratt smiled and wiped sweat from his forehead. 'That's good, Joe, you're talking. Can you feel yourself becoming more lucid?'

'He's never been lucid before, what makes you think he's going to start now?' said Boocock. Idiot. He's a PE teacher—I bet he doesn't even know what lucid means.

'Don't climb back through the window, it's a health and safety issue,' said Pratt. He rifled through his pockets and held up some notes to Mr Groggit. 'Would fifteen quid be enough for a decent ladder?'

'Just call the bloody police,' said Boocock. 'I know some boys on the force who would sort him right out.'

Pratt grabbed Boocock's shoulder. 'No! I can't have the police here again! Did you know we've been front page of the Tammerstone Times three weeks in a row?'

'That's what happens when you have riots,' Boocock drawled.

'How many times do I have to tell you, we do not refer to it as a "riot". It was a "mass altercation",' Pratt snapped. 'Besides, the members of staff involved have all been appropriately disciplined.'

While all this was happening, I was having an idea.

That mat on the ground looked pretty thick. A good half a metre, I thought. Probably quite comfortable. I imagined myself taking off through the air. Feeling a real thrill for the first time in eight months . . . the excitement . . . the adrenaline.

Before I could stop it, the men in the control room in my brain burst into life. Yeah, they're still around.

Do it, said Hank. *What's the worst that could happen?*

Do you REALLY need me to answer that? said Norman, sensible as always. *He could seriously injure himself—he could traumatize his classmates.*

I turned around and saw everyone watching from the window. Mr Shenko looked like he was trying to get everyone to sit down, but they were having none of it. Maybe giving them a little shock wouldn't be such a bad thing. It would definitely make Harry think twice about messing with my stuff again.

Noooo! Norman cried, but it was too late. I grabbed the zombie tight, took a run up, and leapt off the roof.

As soon as I'd done it, I regretted it. The mat suddenly seemed a lot smaller than it did from up there. I was going to have to try to aim for it. I think I took a bit too much of a run up because I seemed to be overshooting.

In fact, I was definitely overshooting. Hurtling through the air, past the mat, and towards the hard ground. Luckily, something broke my fall.

I sat in Mr Pratt's office afterwards, cradling a sugary cup of tea. Pratt had been in and out for a while, probably checking on Boocock in the ambulance. After about half an hour, a woman walked in and sat opposite me. She looked about fifty and was wearing this really hairy jumper and these big, thick bracelets that clacked about when she moved her arms.

'Hello, Joe,' she said. 'My name is Dr Schermerhorn. I am a psychiatrist.'

Oh God.

« Older posts

'Honestly,' I said. 'I don't need a psychiatrist. This was all a big misunderstanding. I was on the roof retrieving my zombie.'

I held it up to Dr Schermerhorn. One of its eyes was hanging down its gutter-blackened face.

Dr Schermerhorn looked at it and nodded slowly. 'Right. Anyway, don't panic. We don't believe you are suicidal, Joe. If you were, you would have picked a much higher roof. We just think that your behaviour has been somewhat erratic of late and that you would benefit from talking to someone about your . . . issues. I have spoken to your mum on the phone . . .'

OH GODDDDD!

'And she has agreed that I should see you once a week. How does that sound?'

I puffed out my cheeks and picked a leaf off the zombie's head. 'Do I have a choice?'

'Not really,' said Dr Schermerhorn. 'See you Wednesday.'

Tuesday 25th June

'I am going to get you, Cowley.' Boocock caught me by my locker after I'd emerged from a quite frankly disastrous History exam. His arm was in a sling and he had a black eye.

'Oh come on, that was an accident,' I said.

He put his face really close to mine. His breath smelled horrible—like someone had dunked a cow poo in a cold cup of coffee. 'No it wasn't,' he hissed. 'You have assaulted me three times now and I have had enough. It is time for revenge.'

I stepped away from the barrage of stinky mouth fumes. 'Give it up, Boocock,' I said. 'The exams are nearly over. I'm practically a free man now. Your powers are useless against me.'

'Oh, I don't mean I'm giving you a detention, or making you do laps,' he said. 'I mean I'm coming for you. I am going to make you SUFFER.'

'Oooh, I'm so scared.' I tried to step around him but he blocked me.

'You should be,' he growled. 'I am a Police Special Constable in my spare time. I've got contacts. I will hunt you down and make you beg for mercy.'

Pfft. Someone's touchy. I don't care if he does get me, anyway. I don't care about anything.

'Did Boocock just threaten you with physical violence, old son?' Harry took his pipe out of his bag. The exam board said he wasn't allowed to take it in with him because he might have been hiding secret notes in there.

'So what if he did?' I said, still narked at him for violating my zombie. 'I hope he strangles me. Put me out of my misery once and for all.'

'Mate, you sound like one of them emus,' said Ad.

Harry gave him a look. They're careful not to mention anything that might remind me of Natalie, but Ad sometimes slips up.

'Sorry,' said Ad. 'But come on, it's been like eight months, ain't it? You should have got over it by now. And you defo shouldn't be jumping off roofs. Have you ever thought you might be one of them bi-polos?'

Harry chuckled. 'Bi-polos. Yes, I've always thought Joe was a massive hole of some sort.'

I dug him in the ribs.

'No, he'll be all right once he's seen all the babes in the VIP area at *BUZZFEST*,' said Ad.

'You're forgetting one minor fact,' I said. 'She's going to be there, too.'

It's true. We each have our own VIP ticket for coming second in the *BUZZFEST* DJ competition last year—me, Harry, Ad, Gav, Natalie, and even that idiot Greeny. I suppose we'll have to go and watch Flossie, the eighty-four-year-old granny who beat us to first place, when she plays the dance stage, to show we're not sore losers. If she lives that long, that is.

'So?' said Ad. 'It's a big place—you can avoid Natalie, can't you?'

We squeezed through the crowd by the doors and out into the car park.

'You must be joking.' Harry took his blazer off and stuffed it into his bag. 'He'll be stalking her around that site like a creepy Sherlock Holmes.'

'No I won't,' I said. 'In fact, forget I said anything. I don't even care about her being there. With that guy who used to be fat. What's his name? Browny?'

'Nah, Greeny,' said Ad.

'What?'

We turned around and saw Greeny standing there. With Natalie. We made eye contact for about a second. Straight away, the control room sprang into life.

Don't say or do anything silly, Joe, said Norman. *Please maintain some dignity.*

WHY DON'T YOU LOVE HIM ANY MORE, YOU HEARTLESS SHREW? Hank screamed. CAN'T YOU SEE WHAT YOU'RE DOING TO HIM? AAAAARRGH!

It's no wonder I can't concentrate with all that going on in my brain. Maybe Dr Schermerhorn can therapize them away.

'Ah hello there, old son,' said Harry. 'Are you up for rehearsals around Ad's tonight?'

'Yeah,' said Greeny. 'Are you coming, Nat?'

'Um . . .' She looked at the floor and tucked a strand of purple hair behind her ear. 'I don't know.'

I sighed. 'I'm not going to be there, Natalie. You'll be fine.'

I totally am going to be there.

9 p.m.

Who needs her, anyway?

9.05 p.m.

I do. God, I really do. I'm walking around the park, trying to calm myself down. I have to record what happened, but that Bible-bashing loon Mad Morris is here and I need to keep my wits about me, so I'm going to use my phone's speech-to-text feature.

9.10 p.m.

I wind two reversal in ass garage. Natalie said you said you worst humming, and I was all, well I chained my mine. She was about to leaf but that tick head Breeny said, no

don't, so she didn't. Anyway, me and Natalie ended up arguing and she started frying and Hairy said you neat two go and coal off. And I said why shut eye? I'm your manager. You cart carrion without me. Meany said actually we've done fine this year without Hugh while you've bin moping around like a depressive.

No, Morris, I don't care about cheeses. Or cod. Well, if I burn in Hull then so be it.

My own Freds have turd a guest me. I ate my wife.

Wednesday 26th June

My first session with Dr Schermerhorn today. I totally didn't want to go. I tried explaining to Mum that I was only on the roof to save a cuddly toy, but she wasn't having any of it. She reckoned that splitting up with Natalie along with Dad leaving us years ago had given me 'abandonment issues'. She reads too many problem pages.

Like I said, I wasn't keen to begin with, but once I properly sat down with Dr Schermerhorn, I changed my mind. She actually listens to me and suggests ways for me to deal with my problems. She said this thing about how negative thoughts can only take hold if I give them power. So basically, I need to stop giving power to the idea of Natalie marrying Greeny and me going mad in the church and going and living in the belfry like some kind of hunchback.

I told her about how I have no friends and that my life is literally over. She asked if my family were supporting me. I told her that my mum had spent the morning whinging at me for not getting my hair cut and saying stuff like, 'I'm not having you looking like a down-and-out on my wedding day.'

The doctor then explained that my hair is a physical representation of my grief and wrote Mum a note saying I should be allowed to have it cut in my own time. When I showed it to her, her mouth went all tight and she muttered something about sending me to one of those boot camps.

Dr Schermerhorn gave me her number so I can call at any time. With the amount of support I get at home, I fear I will need to.

Thursday 27th June

'A Poem for Natalie' by Joseph M. Cowley
My emo love,
Your hand fits mine like a glove.
When you laugh it sounds like a dove.
Actually, no it doesn't.
That would be weird.

Called Dr Schermerhorn and read it to her. She reckons it's good that I'm finding an outlet for my sadness. I asked her if she thought my poem showed promise, but she said she had to go because of an emergency. Probably a mad-man on the loose with a pair of scissors or something.

Friday 28th June

Last exam today. ICT practical. The main question was 'Discuss the advantages and disadvantages of speech-to-text software.' Let's just say I came up with more disad-vantages. I think I did OK, but Boocock was invigilating and kept putting me off by standing at the end of the row and mouthing, 'I'm going to get you,' over and over.

Now I'm home, I've agreed to look after the twins while Mum goes shopping. I'm watching them as they sleep. They're proper amazing, really. They have these tiny little fingers and toes and round, chubby cheeks, and oh God, Ivy's screaming again.

7 p.m.

Mum couldn't get home quick enough as far as I was concerned. I can't tell whether Ivy's still howling or I've got tinnitus.

« Older posts

Anyway, I've just got back from the suit hire place with Jim, Gav, and Jim's best man, Chips. I hate Chips. He's always smoking and has this annoying habit of ruffling my hair and calling me 'Swampy'. Still, I suppose Jim's lucky in a way. He could be like me and have NO FRIENDS AT ALL.

Gav was loving the suit measuring. He had this really nice girl doing him. I had an old bloke who looked like a hobbit Papa Gepetto. And let me tell you something, he was getting that tape measure a little bit too close to my Romulan Neutral Zone, if you know what I mean.

Now the suits are sorted, it feels very real. Soon, my mum is going to be married to a bloke who isn't my dad. Me and Gav are going to be official stepbrothers.

'Hey, Swamps,' said Chips as he lit his seven thousandth cigarette of the day on the way home. 'I bet you're looking forward to this wedding, ain't you? The ushers always get the pick of the wenches.'

'There's only one wench I want,' I said, stroking my recently washed zombie.

'Cheer up, Joe,' said Jim, stopping for a red light. 'Natalie's invited. Who knows? She might give you another chance. Women are always more suggestible at weddings.' He shared a sleazy snigger with Chips. If I find out he met my mother at a wedding, I might actually vomit up my spleen.

'You need to forget about her, blud,' said Gav, ever the sensitive type. 'She's history, you get me?'

'But I love her,' I said.

Gav chuckled. 'Gay.'

Saturday 29th June

Maybe Gav's right. Not about being gay, but about forgetting Natalie.

I mean, just because I'm visiting Doris at Morningside on the day Natalie happens to be working there, doesn't mean I'm going to try to talk to her or anything. No, I'm just going to see Doris. Even though she's Gav's nan. I see her way more than he does. She'll be expecting me. Last time I was there, a week ago today, she was crocheting a lovely vase of flowers. I bet that's nearly done now. Yep, all I'm going to do is pop in, have a look at Doris's crochet, and come home.

3 p.m.

Why can't she love me like she did before? WHY?

4 p.m.

Why?

« Older posts

5 p.m.

She won't even speak to me. It's as if I'm not even there. Why is she punishing me for one mistake? I didn't completely denounce Ad when he told me he thought Klingons were little bits of poo that stuck to your bum hair, so why is she doing this to me?

When I finally got her to talk outside the home, this was what happened.

ME: Hi.

NATALIE: Leave me alone, Joe.

ME: Why won't you talk to me?

NATALIE: Because I've got nothing to say to you.

ME: Come on, let's talk about **STAR TREK**. I watched the one where La Forge kisses that synthesized woman in the Holodeck the other day. It's a good episode, that one.

NATALIE: Look, we can't have what we had before, OK? You hurt me.

ME: But it was a mistake! It's you I really love.

NATALIE: If you loved me, you wouldn't have kissed Lisa.

ME: But it was . . . It was like, an unplanned thing. I was angry about you and Seb. And anyway, she kissed me. I've told you millions of times.

NATALIE: You could have stopped it.

ME: I know, and I wish I did. It's just . . . I fancied her for years, and . . .

NATALIE: You are unbelievable, you know that?

ME: No, I didn't mean it like that.

NATALIE: I'm not going to let you upset me again. Just go away, please.

ME: But, Natalie.

NATALIE: If you had any respect for me whatsoever, you'd do as I say.

Guess who came to walk her home then?

GREENY!

Losing his fat has made him a traitor.

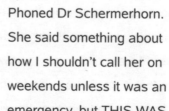

7 p.m.

Phoned Dr Schermerhorn. She said something about how I shouldn't call her on weekends unless it was an emergency, but THIS WAS AN EMERGENCY. She sighed a bit and advised me to breathe deeply and close my eyes. Then she asked me to write a list of words as they popped into my head. Apparently, it would help me to make sense of how I was feeling. This was what I came up with.

Abyss
Despair
Hell
Saveloy (Gav had just been to the chippy)
Degradation

Mum asked what I was writing. I told her to mind her own business, but she wouldn't let it go. In the end, Jim peered over my shoulder and told her he wasn't certain, but it looked like a shopping list for Ikea.

8 p.m.

Just had an idea. Mum and Jim had this show on called Grand Gestures. Basically what happens is that TV presenter bloke with the grey hair who's always shouting goes into a studio audience and bellows someone's name. That person then goes down, sits on a posh settee and talks to him for a bit. Then, Shouty O'Shouterson grins like an imbecile and screams right into their face that someone they know has done something super mad for them to show them how much they care. It's terrible, but I ended up watching it because I have no life.

Anyway, this week, a bloke proposed to his girlfriend, first by hiring a skywriter, then by getting Crazy Vibe, her favourite boyband, to sing a song called 'Marry Me, Baby'.

This is what I've been lacking. Talking is useless. And besides, it's my weakest area. What I need is a Grand Gesture. Some kind of amazing spectacle that will win Natalie's heart back. But what?

9 p.m.

OK, I've just come up with a brilliant idea whilst attempting to untangle my hair from around my retainer. There's nothing that could possibly go wrong with this.

Monday 1st July

'What's this about, anyway?' said Pete Cotterill. He swished his Coke can around on the table and glanced around Griddler's nervously.

'Are you sure you won't have something to eat?' I said. 'I can thoroughly recommend the tuna panini. Mavis in the kitchen is a genius with those things.'

'Just get on with it,' he said. 'I don't exactly want to be seen in a cafe with you.'

'Who cares?' I said. 'School's finished. We're civilians now.'

He shuddered a little bit. I suppose when you're super popular, it must hurt to be thrust into the real world as a regular pleb. Who are you going to lord it over now? I guess this is how PE teachers are created.

« Older posts

'Anyway, the reason I've asked you to meet me here is I have a business proposition for you,' I said.

'What is it, touching up tramps for cash?' he said, with a pathetic smug grin on his face.

'No, you have the monopoly on that, and I don't want to break into your market share,' I replied.

He got up to leave.

'Please, Pete,' I said. 'Just sit down. I'll tell you what the proposition is. It could be beneficial to both of us.'

He adjusted one of his lovingly crafted hair spikes and sat back down. 'Talk.'

'You know you were a member of the school singing club?'

He shrugged as if to say 'duh'.

'And you and a few other guys won the talent show with that boyband thing last year?'

'Yeah, so?'

'Have you ever considered getting the band back together?'

He glared at me for an uncomfortably long time. 'What for?'

'For love, Pete,' I took a sip of my shake. 'For love.'

He blew a raspberry. 'I prefer to work for cash, man.'

I held my hands up. 'Steady on, Jay Zed. I can't offer you money.'

He went to leave again.

'But what I can offer you is even better.'

He stopped.

'I can offer you exposure.'

'What, you want to show me your knob?'

'If it'll help, I will,' I said. 'But that's not what I meant. I mean, I can help you get your name out there as a vocalist.'

He sat down again. 'How can you do that? You're a nobody.'

I tried to laugh all cool-like, but it came out proper loud, like a cow having its udder squeezed too hard. 'If I'm such a nobody, how did I get the SOUND EXPERIENCE to place runner-up in a national DJ competition?' I said. 'And how did I get to number nine in the dance charts as a featured vocal artist?'

'Wasn't that just you saying you're gay over and over again?'

'Oh, I'm sorry,' I said. 'Please, everyone around this table who has had a top ten hit, raise your hand.'

I put my hand up.

'Is everything all right, duck?' Mavis called from the counter.

'Uh, yes, Mavis, I was just stretching my arm.'

'So come on then, Big Time,' said Pete. 'How can you get me noticed?'

I tipped some salt out onto the table and began to mould

it into a J shape with the side of a sugar packet.

'I can see to it that you get a spot as a featured singer on the *SOUND EXPERIENCE*'s next big track.'

Perhaps you shouldn't go making promises you can't keep, Joe, said Norman.

Ah, shut up, Norm. He can talk the guys around on this, said Hank.

Oh yes, we should definitely have faith in Joe's linguistic skills, said Norman. *They've never let us down in the past, have they?*

'All right,' said Pete. 'You've got a deal.'

'Excellent,' I said. 'Get your guys together. I'm going to need all of you. While you're doing that, I'll source the costumes.'

'Costumes?' he said. 'You didn't say anything about costumes.'

'Hey,' I said. 'There are plenty of singers out there who'd love to work in my organization. So are you in or out?'

He sighed. 'All right, I'm in.'

This is going to be brilliant.

Tuesday 2nd July

Have you ever tried feeding a baby? Shovelling spag bol into Ad's gob when he broke his wrists last year is beginner level stuff in comparison. I just don't have the knack for it. Even Gav is better at it than me. My attempt at feeding this morning ended with Ivy smacking the bowl onto the floor and laughing right in my face.

Thinking about it, Ivy is definitely more like Gav—loud, destructive, smelly. Holly is like me—quiet, slightly whiny, has crap hair. I know you shouldn't pick favourites when it comes to babies but there we are.

Anyway, I had more important things to worry about than getting mashed-up banana spat all over me—like how I was going to get these outfits for my Grand Gesture. A year ago, I could have borrowed them from the wardrobe department at Greeny's dad's low budget film studio, but since he basically stole Natalie from me, stuff has gone sour. I need to turn on the charm if this is going to be a success.

7 p.m.

Oh, Joe Cowley, you have the wit and sophistication of James Bond himself. This is what happened:

I arrived at Greeny's house when I was sure his parents would be at work.

'Oh, hello,' he said. 'Can I, like, help?'

'Just checking in, mate,' I said.

He ran his hand down his front. He's always doing that. It's as if he needs to remind himself that he's no longer fat.

'But you never check in,' he said. 'And you definitely never call me mate.'

'I know,' I said. 'But I'm the manager of the

$SOUND\ EXPERIENCE$, and I've realized I need to take more interest in the talent.'

Greeny's eyes darted around a bit. 'Fine.'

We walked into his kitchen. It was way bigger than the one in my house. They had well fancy stuff, too, like one of those machines that makes tiny cups of coffee. A load of old motor parts lay on the marble-effect work surface next to a half-drunk Slim Fast. He must have noticed me looking.

'Just an old camera,' he said with a shrug. 'I like to take stuff apart, see how it works.'

'Great,' I said, all the while thinking, I'd love to take YOU apart to see how YOU work, you turncoat. 'So . . . are you doing anything later? Seeing anybody?'

He took a sip of his shake and frowned at me. 'Don't know,' he said. 'Maybe.'

Ooh, you cute little jackass, said Hank.

'What are you really doing here, Joe?' said Greeny. 'I reckon you've got anterior motives.'

'Wha? I have no ulterior motives being here,' I said. 'If you want to hang around with my ex-girlfriend as friends then that's no business of mine. As friends . . . You are just friends, aren't you?'

He tutted and started fiddling with the knackered camera.

'Anyway, anyway,' I said. 'Enough about that. Natalie is free to do what she likes. No, I was wondering if I could have a look in your dad's costume store?'

He looked up from his work. 'Why?'

'I've had an idea about an alternate look for the $SOUND$ $EXPERIENCE$, and I just wanted to see if you had it.'

He shrugged. 'I suppose so, but the three of us are happy with the way things are.'

The three of us? I'm part of that three, not him. Stealing my girl and now my friends? One of these days, I'm going to come home to find him sleeping in my cocking bed.

We went through to the big costume store. It's double the size of a normal garage and has huge wall-to-wall rails full of weird outfits. I knew he had what I was after in there because I had seen it before. I just couldn't remember where exactly.

'What are you looking for, anyway?' he said.

'Oh, just something,' I replied, rifling through labelled suit bags. 'I'll know it when I see it.'

He grunted then started doing jumping jacks. God, he's never off, is he?

Greeny's dad must be super organized because I quickly found the designated sci-fi rail. I worked my way along, past Cybermen and Stormtroopers until I finally saw the Starfleet Combadge glinting back at me. Bingo.

I sifted through. All four were there.

Control room: what do I do now?

I would advise asking Greeny if you could borrow them, said Norman.

Belay that, my man, said Hank. *Belay that until the freakin' cows come home. Just think about it for a sec— who else does he know who's into Star Trek? As soon as you go, he's going to tell Natalie you borrowed the Starfleet uniforms and blow the whole thing.*

So what are you saying, Hank?

I'm saying you have to take them without him knowing.

Page 37 of 272 »

Isn't that basically burglary? said Norman.

Potayto, potahto, said Hank.

There was no way I'd be able to get those uniforms past Greeny. What was I going to do? Stick them up my shirt and say, 'Hey, I found all that fat you lost'?

I needed another way. I looked around. No ideas. Until something caught my eye. A small window near the ceiling. I could shove the uniforms through that and grab them when I got outside. But I had to get Mr Jazzercise out of the room.

'Found it yet?'

'Not yet,' I lied. 'Hey, what kind of host are you, anyway? You haven't offered me a drink.'

He huffed. 'What do you want?'

'How about a cup of tea?' I said. 'And leave the bag in for a looooong time. I like it strong.'

He tutted and walked out. As soon as he was out of earshot, I grabbed the four uniforms and laid them on the floor, out of sight. The window was too high for me to reach on my own. I had to improvise.

I pushed an old flowery armchair up against the wall as quietly as I could.

'Do you want sugar?'

I nearly screamed when Greeny appeared in the doorway. I quickly sat down in the chair in an attempt to look super casual.

« Older posts

'N-no, I'm sweet enough. Ha HAAA!'

Super. Casual.

Greeny shook his head and walked back out. Once I could hear clattering in the kitchen, I jumped up, grabbed the uniforms, and climbed onto the chair. It creaked ominously and wobbled as if one of the legs was shorter than the others. Working fast, I lumped the heavy costumes onto one arm and used the other hand to wrench open the window as far as it would go. I tried to shove them through but they wouldn't fit. They'd have to go one at a time.

A yellow one went through first. Then the grey. I heard a drawer close in the kitchen so I balled the other yellow one up and tossed it out like a basket-ball. The creaking of the chair beneath me became a groan. The claret one was halfway through when the Combadge got snagged on the handle. My head pounded. I couldn't have Greeny catching me like this. Footsteps clomped down the corridor. I yanked it off and shoved it out.

Before I could jump off, one of the chair legs snapped completely and I clattered to the floor, whacking the same shoulder I bruised on the school roof.

I lay on the ground, trying to suck some air back into my lungs.

'What are you doing?'

'Lying down, what does it look like?' I puffed.

Greeny slammed the mug down on a chest of drawers and folded his arms.

'Yeah, sorry.' I winced as I sat up. 'I was just trying to peek on top of that wardrobe to see if there was anything up there, but the chair broke. Don't worry. I won't sue.'

I'd normally feel guilty about lying like that, but when you're plotting a Grand Gesture, you gotta do what you gotta do.

'Right,' he said.

'Yes,' I said. 'Anyway, you haven't got what I was after, so I'll be off. It was nice seeing you, Greeny.'

'But you haven't drunk your tea.'

'Bye then!' I said, and got out of there before he noticed the open window.

I walked down the street in case he was watching me, then doubled back, ducking behind hedges. When I got to his house again, I crept up the side and found the uniforms crumpled on the ground. I quickly rolled them up and carried them home without being seen.

Part of me feels bad about nicking Greeny's costumes, but then I remember that he nicked the love of my life and I tell that part of me to shut its face.

« Older posts

I have the four uniforms laid out on my bunk. My personal Picard special is hanging in the wardrobe. The Grand Gesture is another step closer to completion. I've never orchestrated a scheme on my own before and so far it is going flawlessly.

Maybe this is the dawning of a new me. Perhaps I am a grubby little caterpillar who is going to emerge from his cocoon as a self-possessed, confident, handsome young butterfly who isn't afraid to get out there and take what he wants.

Anyway, I'd better stop cos I need to put my retainer on.

Wednesday 3rd July

I sat in Dr Schermerhorn's waiting room, preparing myself for another hour inside the smouldering wreckage that is my psyche. I thought our first session and subsequent ten phone calls had been really helpful and I was feeling more confident, and as I mentioned last night, butterfly-like. It was time to delve deeper.

The door opened. Here we go.

'Um, Joe Cowley?'

I looked up. That was not Dr Schermerhorn. For one, he was male, and two, he was about thirty years younger.

I got up and followed him into the office.

'Are you, like, Dr Schermerhorn's secretary, or something?'

The man pointed at a seat and chuckled. 'No, Joe, my name is Troy. I am your new therapist.'

I stopped and gawped at him.

'Wait, what?' I cried. 'What happened to Dr Schermerhorn?'

Troy smiled soothingly as he sat down and crossed his skinny legs. 'It's OK, Joe. Dr Schermerhorn has moved on.'

'Moved on? Why?' I couldn't believe what I was hearing. All my butterfly-like feelings disappeared. I was more like an idiot moth, flapping around a lightbulb and flying full-whack into closed windows.

'It doesn't matter, Joe,' he said. 'Please sit.'

I plonked myself down in the chair. 'But I had her phone number! I could call her any time! Can I do that with you?'

Troy smiled. 'No. But I have made you something that will help.'

He passed me a USB stick.

'What's this?'

'It's a collection of chill-out music,' he said. 'Whenever you feel anxious, just pop it on and it will relax you. I created it myself.'

I yanked a tissue out of the box and started tearing it up into tiny pieces. 'I don't get why she's gone. We seemed to be making good progress.'

Troy clasped his hands together and formed a pistol shape with his fingers, which he used to rest his chin on. It was then I noticed his nose. It was truly enormous. Like a shark's fin sticking out of his face. The more I tried to avoid looking at it, the more it seemed to follow me around the room. I swear, I could almost hear the *Jaws* music.

'Does this make you feel angry?' he asked.

I blinked hard and tried to stop thinking about sharks. 'You bet your arse it does, matey,' I said. 'I mean, no offence, but how old are you?'

Troy dissolved his double-handed pistol and gripped the arms of his chair. 'We're not here to talk about me, we're here to talk about you. Now according to the notes Dr Schermerhorn left me, you were having some trouble getting over a break-up?'

I huffed. 'Who even are you, Troy? And why is your name Troy and not doctor something? Dr Schermerhorn had her credentials on the wall. You have a canvas of a tin of soup. Where are your credentials? I want to see your CREDENTIALS.'

'Joe,' Troy said, his voice wavering. 'I have already told you, this session is not about me. Now come on, let's start.'

'Not until I see some credentials,' I said. 'I mean, how do I know you're not some whackadoodle who has Dr Schermerhorn tied up in the boot of his car, and is going to kill me and wear my face like a Halloween mask? Huh? How do I know you're not THAT?'

Troy sighed and reached into his drawer. 'Here,' he said and threw a certificate down on the table. I read it, then looked up at him with disgust.

'You're a counsellor?' I said. 'A cocking counsellor? Dr Schermerhorn was an actual therapist. You're just some bloke from the bloody Samaritans!'

Troy rubbed his eyes. 'I can assure you that I am not "just some bloke from the bloody Samaritans" as you put it. I am fully trained to deal with your problems.'

I got up out of my chair and started pacing in front of the window. I walked so quickly, my hair kept flicking into my mouth.

'OK, well let me ask you this,' I said. 'How would you feel if you had to have your tonsils out, and they wheeled you down to theatre, but instead of a surgeon, there was a plumber?'

'I don't think that's an appropriate analogy,' said Troy.

'"Ooh, I'm fully trained," the plumber says. "I mean what is the throat if not a fleshy U-bend? Nurse, pass the plunger."'

'ENOUGH,' Troy snapped.

I stopped pacing.

'Dr Schermerhorn has been moved on due to budget cuts. The health authority can no longer afford a licensed psychiatrist, so they're having to use counsellors instead. Happy now?'

I took a deep breath. 'Well clearly not, otherwise I wouldn't be here, would I?'

Troy quietly counted to ten. 'Please sit, Joe,' he said. 'Because it's either me or nothing.'

I looked around the office. Could I really sort out my problems by myself? Probably not. I walked back to the chair and sat down.

'Fine,' I said. 'Fix my brain, Troy.'

Thursday 4th July

Well, that was weird. Troy made me sit there and write a letter to my younger self, giving advice on what to do and what mistakes to avoid. I told him it was a stupid idea that a stupid person would come up with, but he insisted. Here is what I wrote:

Dear young Joe,

I am writing you this letter from the future. Don't freak out. It's not that big a deal. We don't have flying cars, or transporters that can beam us anywhere in the universe. To be honest, it's pretty much the same as your era except the internet is faster. What I'm trying to say is, the future is rubbish.

And it's not just technology, young Joe. Our personal life is a disaster area—I mean, we are being given counselling by some nine year old called Troy for cocking out loud—so here's what I want you to do to save us from this awful fate.

1. Stop obsessing about Lisa Hall. Seriously, she is nothing but bad news. Yes, we did get to snog her, but the price we paid was NOT worth it.

2. Find a girl called Natalie Tuft. She is the best. Never let her go.

3. Don't try to stop our parents from divorcing. I know this might sound weird, but they are happier apart. At least I think they are.

4. You know how that Gav kid is always giving us a hard time? Yeah, get used to that.

5. Soon, Harry and Ad are going to invite you into their 'tree house'. Do NOT go in. It is far from structur-

ally sound.

6. Invent something called 'twerking'. It is a dance where you wave your arse about. You will be rich and famous.

7. Don't go into therapy because they will eventually replace your doctor with some berk who makes you write stupid letters to yourself.

Yours sincerely,
You (aged 16)

When I finished, I asked Troy what I should do with the letter. He huffed and said, 'Oh, I think you know exactly what you can do with it.'

Friday 5th July

Spent most of the day at Pete Cotterill's house. Which is a sentence I never thought I'd write. The boyband is now fully assembled. I don't know any of them that well, but here is a dossier of the facts I have at hand:

- **Pete Cotterill:** Douche. Sings all day as if girls find that irresistible. Which apparently they do.
- **Darren Ward:** Douche. Reckons he's really tough, but I totally saw him crying when he broke his leg playing rugby.
- **Jamal Chauhan:** Douche. One time, when I pointed out that we have the same initials, he just tutted and said,

'Yeah well so does Jesus Christ, but I ain't lending him a quid either.' Also, a cheapskate.

- **Jordan Foster:** Douche. Although the way he crapped himself in Year Three and managed to live it down is nothing short of a modern miracle.

Trouble is, I've now had to promise that all of them will get to sing on a 𝕊OUND EXPERIENCE song. Who knows? Maybe I'll invent a new musical genre: boyband-step.

God, the 𝕊OUND EXPERIENCE are going to kill me, aren't they?

Anyway, I need to forget about them for now. The important thing is getting the Grand Gesture just right. I can deal with the fallout later.

I gave Cotterill's quartet a copy of the song I want them to sing: 'Us Against the Universe' by Oh, Inverted World. It's Natalie's favourite song by her favourite band.

'Sounds like emo crap to me,' said Jordan.

'Yes, I know it does,' I said. 'But it has special sentimental value and it's important that you convey that in your singing.'

'What if I don't want to?'

'Then you don't get to perform with the country's hottest new dance act,' I shot back.

He cracked his knuckles and my intestines started quivering. Luckily, he just tutted and went back to reading the lyrics, rather than ripping out my pelvis and wearing it like a party hat.

They listened to it a few times, then started working on their arrangement. Pete was actually very good at this. Not that I'd ever admit that to him. He looks pleased enough with himself as it is.

'Anyway, what are these costumes you've got for us?' said Pete.

'Starfleet uniforms,' I replied.

'What the hell's that?' said Darren.

'You know, from **STAR TREK**,' I said.

'No way—I ain't wearing no geek clothes,' said Jamal.

'Hey, don't forget, JC, I can easily replace you,' I said. 'Remember Pete Best from the Beatles?'

'No.'

'Exactly,' I said. 'Anyway, it's not all that geeky. Let me explain who you're going to be playing.'

I took out a sheet I'd prepared which outlined the various characters.

Joe: Captain Picard
The mastermind. Delegates to other crew members but isn't afraid to get his hands dirty.

Pete: Data

Second officer and sentient, fully functional android. You'll be playing him because you're the lead singer and Data is Natalie's favourite character. Behind Picard, of course.

Jamal: Geordi La Forge
Chief engineer. Born blind but wears a VISOR to give him sight. (You can borrow mine but for the love of God be careful with it.)

Darren: Wesley Crusher
Helmsman. Kind of annoying.

Jordan: William T. Riker
First officer of the USS Enterprise. To be honest, I've only picked you to be him because you're biggest. If you could draw a beard on your face, that would be great, but if not, we'll just say you're series one Riker.

They seem to be going with it for now. I'm not looking forward to telling Pete he has to paint himself grey, though. One thing at a time.

Saturday 6th July

After visiting Doris (Natalie avoided me the entire time), I went to the joke shop in town to buy a bald cap for my

« Older posts

Picard transformation.

While I was there, I picked up a fake spider to get Gav with later. He is proper scared of spiders but won't admit it. Once, he claimed to have run out of the bathroom naked and screaming because the mirror was haunted. He would rather admit to that than to arachnophobia. Thought about getting some fart powder as well, but increasing Gav's flatulence capabilities would probably create a rip in the space-time continuum/the seat of his pants.

10.30 p.m.
OK, I've put the spider on his pillow. Now to play the waiting game.

11.30 p.m.
Still waiting.

12.15 a.m.
Getting sleepy.

Sunday 7th July
Turns out Gav was staying over with his mates the Blenkinsops last night. Always two steps ahead.

Spent the day at Dad's. He and his about-ninety-years-younger-than-him Russian fiancée, Svetlana, are now planning for their wedding next year. God help me. Apparently, I'm going to be best man, and Hercules the rat dog is going to be a ring bearer. I noticed Svetlana looking at dresses in a magazine. They were ALL terrible. Like Doris's toilet roll doll crossed with a mirror ball.

When Svetlana went to the hairdresser's for her weekly style, Dad stood up and started pacing around. I was just getting to level eighty-nine on *Furious Feathers* and it was really distracting.

'What's up?' I said, not looking up from my phone.

Dad stopped and sighed. 'Can I talk to you for a minute, son?'

'Yep,' I said.

'Without the phone.'

I huffed and exited the game. It's fine—I didn't want to earn a Gold Feather anyway.

'Your mum's wedding,' he said. 'Everything's . . . all right isn't it?'

He stared at me, chewing his lip. It was weird. He was using normal sentences without any hip-hop slang or anything.

'Um yeah, it's OK,' I said.

« Older posts

'No, I mean, it is what she wants, isn't it?'

Huh? I consulted the control room for advice but they were no help.

Man, I prefer him when he's playing gangsta rap from his phone, said Hank.

'Well, I would have thought so,' I said. 'I mean, Jim isn't forcing her to marry him against her will.'

Dad stopped chewing his lip and shook his head. 'Yeah, you're right,' he said. 'Forget I even said anything.'

'What?' I said.

'Never mind, dawg, it's just your daddy-o being a jive-ass turkey.'

Awesome, he's back, said Hank.

Ran into one of the Blenkinsops on the way home and asked how the sleepover went last night and if they did each other's nails. I really have no regard for my own safety any more. Anyway, long story short—he knew nothing about a sleepover. Which means Gav wasn't there.

I went to ask Gav where he was, but he gave me a dead arm for leaving a plastic spider on his pillow. Some pranks just aren't worth it.

10 p.m.

Noticed I'm missing a significant amount of my aftershave. This is not good. When Natalie takes me back after the

Grand Gesture I'm going to need to be smelling fresh.

I know it must be Gav or Jim who's taking it, but I need to catch them in the act. I'm going to set my webcam up on the shelf so I have evidence.

Monday 8th July

Took the costumes over to Pete's for fitting. None of them seemed happy about it, but the carrot of a *SOUND EXPERIENCE* guest slot is still enough to keep them all onside. We did a dress rehearsal and they're sounding good. This is going to be excellent.

5 p.m.

I've reviewed the camera footage and it's as I suspected: Gav is the phantom aftershave thief. I am in possession of video footage of him spraying it on his face, neck, wrists,

chest, and down his pants, followed by several minutes of him yowling in pain. I think it's time for a confrontation.

7 p.m.

'Looking for something?' I spun around on my computer chair as Gav walked in. I'd been rehearsing that for ages. I stroked my stuffed zombie like a cat.

'What you on about?'

'Oh, I don't know,' I said. 'My aftershave, perhaps?'

Gav's eyes darted around the room. 'You're a mentalist. And that thing you're wearing on your face don't exactly help.'

'It's called a retainer—look it up,' I snapped. 'And anyway, stop trying to change the subject, because I have incontrovertible proof that you have been pilfering my Steve Saint Laurence.' (I bought it down the market for a fiver.)

'Whatevs. I'll get you some more when I get paid, innit?'

I scooched the chair closer to him.

'I think we both know that isn't going to happen, don't we?' I said. 'Now come on, why have you been doing it? What's her name?'

'What you on about?' he said. 'I just wear it for work, innit?'

'You wear my aftershave to go and work in a ware-house?' I said. 'A bit of a waste, don't you think?'

'All right, I won't do it again,' he said. 'Can I go now, Mother?'

I eyeballed him. Something wasn't right about the way he was acting.

'Yes,' I said. 'You're free to go. For now.'

He tutted and stomped out.

He's seeing a girl—that much is clear. But why the secrecy? Why wouldn't he want me to know about her?

Oh God. It's Natalie isn't it? I've been worried about Greeny when it's Gav I should have been watching.

Don't be silly, Joe, said Norman. *You have absolutely no reason to believe they would be an item.*

Why not? said Hank. *They get along just fine. And why else would he be so cagey? If I were you I'd trail him next time he leaves the house. Go on a stake-out.*

Don't be ridiculous, Hank, said Norman. *He would never do something so foolish, would you, Joe?*

Joe?

Tuesday 9th July

Stakeout equipment

Phone CHECK

Light coat in case of rain CHECK

Torch in case of night-time surveillance CHECK

« Older posts

Bag of crisps CHECK

Capri-Sun pouch CHECK

I'm ready to go. What I discover may be painful, but at least it will be the truth.

9 p.m.

Stakeout results:

Inconclusive.

Reasons:

Gav realized I was following him when I tripped over a small dog and yelled, 'Jesus cocking Christ.'

Outcome:

A dead leg and a threat that if I follow him again, he'll 'mash my face up'.

Wednesday 10th July

I noticed Troy had all his credentials framed on his wall today. Even his GCSEs and Duke of Edinburgh Awards, which seemed like overkill to me.

'Now, Joe,' he said as I sat down opposite him. 'I feel that we got off on the wrong foot last time, so we should start again. Agreed?'

I huffed. 'Fine.' I guessed my letter to the Health Secretary, urging him to reinstate Dr Schermerhorn, had ended up in the government shredder.

'So,' Troy went on. 'Are there any issues you'd particularly like to discuss today?'

'Loads,' I said. 'For one thing, I now officially suspect my stepbrother of having a fling with my ex.'

Troy flicked through his notes. 'Is this Lisa you're referring to?'

I tutted. 'No, not that ex—Natalie. The love of my life, Natalie! God, keep up, Troy.'

Troy seemed to be gritting his teeth.

'Oh, and that "chill-out" music you gave me was crap, too.'

He looked up at me, shocked. 'What do you mean?'

'It was BORING,' I said. 'When I listened to it, it basically sent me to sleep!'

'But that's the whole—'

'Anyway,' I said, cutting in. 'I've been watching my stepbrother, looking out for telltale clues. Black lipstick on and around his face, purple hairs on his clothes. I even took his phone off the bedside table and tried to read his messages.'

'Joe, this behaviour is deeply unhealthy,' said Troy.

'Whatever, it was PIN protected anyway. And when I tried to guess it, a message saying "try again and I'll kill you" flashed up.'

Troy rubbed his chin. 'I think we need to delve deeper into this issue.'

'Too cocking right we do,' I said. 'Do you know any good ways of spying on people?'

Troy sighed. 'I didn't mean that. I mean we need to examine why you're feeling this way.'

I gawped at him. 'Um, duh! Because I suspect the two of them of having a thing behind my back.'

Troy stood up and walked to the other side of the room. He came back carrying a small plastic chair with a doll sitting on it.

'Well, this is marvellous,' I said. 'The love of my life won't talk to me and you want me to replace her with a doll? I'm beginning to think you made that certificate on Paint.'

Troy put the chair down and pointed at the doll. 'That is your father,' he said.

I stared at it. It was a baby in a romper suit.

'I'm pretty sure it isn't, Troy.'

He sat back down opposite me. 'For the purposes of this exercise it is,' he said. 'I want you to talk to the doll as if it is your dad. Tell him how he has let you down and made you into the person you are today.'

I scowled at him. 'What are you on about? I've not even mentioned my dad.'

'You didn't have to,' he said. 'Everything is linked to the subconscious and I believe that your parents' divorce and your relationship with your father has had a disastrous effect on your mental well-being.'

I folded my arms. 'You're way off the mark with this one, Troy Wonder.'

Troy took a massive book out of his desk and opened it at a bookmarked page. 'Children with divorced parents often display signs of insecurity . . .'

Check, said Hank.

'. . . anxiety . . .'

Check, said Norman.

'. . . and can sometimes be argumentative and abusive.'

'I am NOT argumentative and abusive, you weasel-faced dog penis.'

Troy raised his eyebrows at me.

'OK, fine, I'll talk to the stupid doll,' I said, turning around to face it. 'What am I supposed to say?'

'Just let it out, Joe,' said Troy. 'Tell your father all the ways he disappoints or embarrasses you.'

It had to be worth a go, I supposed.

'Um.' I scratched my cheek and pondered. 'Y-you have a stupid hairdo. You're too old for it.'

« Older posts

'Good,' said Troy. 'But let's go deeper—beyond the superficial.'

'Your taste in music is crap?'

'Deeper.'

'Sometimes, when I hear you use rapping slang in public, I'm so embarrassed that I tell people you're my uncle who got brain damaged in a car accident.'

'Deeper still,' said Troy. 'Think about when you were a small child. What did he do that shaped who you are today?'

'Um, I don't know.'

'You do, Joe,' he said, urging me on. 'It's in there, gnawing away at your subconscious. Think really hard. If we can get it out in the open, we could have the key to your recovery.'

I thought about it. I relived all the embarrassing things Dad ever did to me—all the times he made me feel sad. There were so many that I struggled to pick one, but suddenly, something resurfaced. Something huge—like an iceberg jutting out of a calm ocean. My stomach quivered, my heart pounded.

JOE'S DAD

'I've got it,' I whispered.

'Excellent,' said Troy. 'Come on, tell him how his actions hurt you. Cleanse your psyche!'

I stared into the vacant eyes of the doll. 'Y-you told me that **STAR TREK**: The Next Generation would never be as good as **STAR TREK**: The Original Series and that Picard is a second-rate Kirk.' I stopped and shook my head in disbelief—the memory raw and painful again, like knocking off a scab before the wound has healed. 'Um, hello? Picard is the complete captain—assured, dedicated, and restrained, but not afraid of getting physical if need be. A second-rate Kirk? Have you ever heard anything so stupid in all your life, Troy?'

He didn't answer.

'Troy?'

I looked up at him. He had his head in his hands.

I didn't realize what I had uncovered was so powerful.

Thursday 11th July

Headed off for the final rehearsal before the Grand Gesture. It was then I dropped the bomb about the whole being painted grey thing.

'You never mentioned anything about that before,' said Pete.

'I didn't think I had to,' I said. 'Everybody knows Data is grey.'

'Yeah, well I didn't,' said Pete.

'None of us did, 'cause we ain't freaks,' said Jamal.

'You know, I was talking to the *SOUND EXPERIENCE* guys

« Older posts

today,' I said, which was a lie because I haven't spoken to them since Harry kicked me out of rehearsals. 'And they said they've written a track that would be great for you guys. They say it's going to be an even bigger hit than "Gay as the Day Is Long".'

The boyband exchanged a series of glances.

'All right, where's this paint then?' said Pete.

9 p.m.

Gav is out again. I sat on my bunk and logged onto InstaMsg. Natalie was online.

There is all the proof you need, said Norman. *If she was with Gav, she wouldn't be on here.*

Maybe that's right, said Hank. *But you should talk to her, just to be safe.*

No, don't do that, said Norman. *No, no, no.*

Shut down control room communications.

Hi. X

Natalie is typing . . .

Natalie is typing . . .

Natalie is typing . . .

Hi.

It took her five minutes to write that? What was going on?

Everything OK?

Yep. Busy.

Busy molesting Gav?

I thought I had shut down control room communications.

Busy doing what?

I didn't realize I had to tell you everything I was doing. But if you must know, I'm chatting to someone else.

Who?

JOE! Can't you at least try to be a bit grown up?

OK, I'm sorry.

. . .

Is it Greeny?

I'm going.

Natalie is offline.

Damn. Still, as soon as she sees my Grand Gesture tomorrow, she's going to fall in love with me all over again, I guarantee it.

Friday 12th July

Everything was perfect.

I arrived at Pete's house already wearing my Picard uniform and bald cap and helped apply the grey paint to his face and hands. Then he slicked back his spikes. If you squinted, he really did look like Data. I gave Jamal my VISOR to finish off his

« Older posts

La Forge costume and added a couple of finishing touches to the other two. I stood back and admired my handiwork. We made a pretty convincing crew. We certainly wouldn't disgrace ourselves at a Con.

'Gentlemen, let's do this,' I said. 'Engage.'

They all stared at me.

'You're such a bender,' said Riker.

'There's no need for personal insults, Number One,' I said.

'I can't believe we have to walk all the way across town dressed like this,' said Wesley Crusher. 'This track had better be good.'

'Believe me, it's the best,' I said.

Heckles heard en route to Natalie's house

Beam me up, Scotty: 15

Live long and prosper: 10

Make it so: 2

Freaks: 37

The people of Tammerstone are philistines.

I stopped paying attention after a while. My mind was totally focused on the task at hand. I visualized it. Natalie would come to her window and see my lovingly crafted representations of her favourite song and favourite TV show and would instantly be reminded that we are true soulmates. Then she would run downstairs and we'd kiss just as the quartet got to the crescendo of the song. Maybe it would even start raining. It was going to be the best thing ever. A Hollywood ending.

'IS THAT YOU, COWLEY?'

My perfect rom-com scenario skidded off the reel and was replaced by a dystopian apocalypse disaster snuff movie.

'Oh crap, it's Boocock!'

I sprinted in the opposite direction, away from the crazy Special Constable PE teacher. For some reason, the others ran too, probably because of crimes they still hadn't been punished for.

'You can't run from me forever!' he screamed after us.

'That's where you're wrong, Boocock,' I shouted back. 'Thanks to all those laps you made me do, I now have incredible stamina.'

He had no way of knowing I felt like I was about to pass out.

I wondered why no one on the street was doing anything to help this gang of innocent Trekkers being chased by a maniac. Then I remembered that he was in a PCSO uniform and they must have thought we were the world's geekiest criminal gang.

I turned down an alleyway that I knew led to the wooded area on the edge of the park. I thought I could lose him in there. The others followed. I didn't know much longer I'd be able to keep the pace.

'This is resisting arrest!' Boocock screamed at us, as if he were an actual police officer. His arm was just bandaged and not in a sling. This was not good news.

Pete and I ducked behind a thick hedge and watched Boocock blunder past, still screaming my name. We had lost the other three somewhere along the way. My heart pounded. I felt like a fox being chased by an army of inbred poshos on horseback. When Boocock said he was going to get me, I never took him seriously.

After he had run back the way he came, still searching for me, we crept out from behind the bush and carried on through the trees to the big hill on the other side of the park that overlooked Natalie's house. My calves burned as we climbed past a bloke walking his dogs. He didn't even look at us twice. Clearly, Captain Picard and Data legging it past you is nothing out of the ordinary in that part of town.

I ran down the hill and into Natalie's back garden. I stopped, gripped my knees, and tried to force some air back into my lungs.

'You can't think we're still doing this?' said Pete, panting.

'Oh yes we are,' I said.

I pulled out my phone and called Jordan.

'What?' he grunted, sounding as out of breath as me.

'Where are you?'

'Going home,' he said.

'Well, get back here,' I said. 'You've got a job to do, remember?'

'Are you off your nut?' he said. 'That mental PE teacher is after us.'

'But—'

He hung up. Damn.

I turned to Pete. 'Looks like it's just you now.'

'No way,' he said. 'I'm not doing it on my own.'

'Hey.' I poked him in the chest. 'I'm your boss and I say you have to work.'

He poked me back. 'You ain't my boss, and if you touch me again, there's going to be trouble.'

'Oh really?' I said, anger boiling in my guts like tar. 'Well maybe I want some trouble.'

I poked him again, harder.

'That's it.'

« Older posts

Pete shoved me to the ground and started punching me in the stomach. It was painful, both physically and emotionally, because the last person who punched me in the stomach was Natalie. Fast as I could, I replied with a thump of my own and knocked the wind out of him.

Sensing an advantage, I climbed on top and held his arms down with my knees. I couldn't quite bring myself to hit him properly so I just kept slapping him around the cheeks. Really quick ones, like an angry penguin.

'Get off me, you queer,' he yelled.

I gave him a few more stingers around the face and dug in harder with my knees.

'Hey, what the hell are you doing?'

I stopped slapping for a second and looked up. Natalie stood there, watching out of her bedroom window, her mouth open in an expression of horrified fury.

'Oh God, is that you, Joe?'

Say no, said Hank. *Say no and run like the freakin' wind!*

It's no good, Joe, said Norman. *She knows it's you.*

'Y-yes it is,' I mumbled.

She didn't say anything. Pete even stopped kicking underneath me.

'I . . . I did this for you,' I said.

As soon as the words left my mouth, I had one of those out-of-body experiences. It was as if I were looking down on myself from above, seeing things as Natalie was. Apparently, this amazing thing I had done for her was trespass on her property dressed as Captain Picard, then sit on Data and bitch-slap him until his grey face turned pink.

'Why would you think I'd want to see this?' she said.

I didn't have an answer. How could everything have gone so wrong? This was supposed to be our Hollywood moment. My Grand Gesture working its miraculous magic. What it ended up as was the world's wimpiest geek fight.

'I don't know,' I said. 'I just don't know any more.'

She shook her head. 'I want you out of my garden, Joe.

« Older posts

Now. I really don't want to call the police, but I will if you don't leave.'

'What's up?'

My blood froze. Someone walked behind her and put his arm around her shoulder. Greeny.

I jumped to my feet. 'Oh, well this is just MARVELLOUS! When we were going out, you wouldn't let me in your house for SIX MONTHS. But there he is: RIGHT IN THERE!'

'You don't know what you're talking about,' Natalie said, her teeth clenched.

'Oh, don't I?' I screamed. 'Well, get a load of this: you were never interested in him when he was fat, were you?'

'Joe, I—'

'Save it,' I said. 'I thought you were different, but it turns out you're just as shallow as the rest of them. I hope you're really happy together.'

Natalie put her hand to her mouth and walked away.

'And by the way,' I cried, 'I don't hope you're happy together at all. I meant that last bit SARCASTICALLY.'

Pete got up and skulked off.

'I think you need to go,' said Greeny.

'I'm going nowhere,' I said, scooping up clods of mud and chucking them at him with terrible aim. 'You stinking backstabber.'

'Hey,' he said. 'Where did you get those Starfleet uniforms?'

'All right, I'm going.'

God, I'm such a knob. Why did I say those things to Natalie? I didn't mean any of them. I've texted her saying sorry but she hasn't replied. If I'm going to put this right, I'll need the Grandest Gesture the world has ever seen.

Saturday 13th July

Dear Sirs,

I am writing to you to complain about the conduct of one of your Police Community Support Officers, Mr Boocock. I'm afraid I don't know his first name, and I'm sure rumours that it is 'Moocock' are false.

Anyway, I believe he has a personal vendetta against me. Just yesterday, he chased me down the high street screaming for my blood. I should point out at this juncture that I have committed no criminal offences and a check of my record will bear this out.

I'll finish this later because I've just got a text from Harry:

Sound Experience meeting. Griddler's at 2. Your presence is required.

Finally, they're ready to take me back.

4.30 p.m.

How could I have ever called these people friends? I am doomed. Destined to walk this earth alone like a leper, or

Mad Morris on a hot day.

As soon as I arrived at Griddler's, I knew something was up: Harry, Ad, Greeny, and Natalie were sitting at a big table—the four of them crammed into one side, meaning I had to sit opposite. None of them would look me in the eye.

'Do you want a chip, Joe?' Ad pointed at a bowl in the middle of the table.

'No thanks,' I said. 'So what's up? Am I allowed back into the fold? Because if I am, there are going to be some changes.'

'Not exactly, old boy,' said Harry. 'I, um, the thing is . . .' He stopped and rubbed his forehead. 'I can't do it.'

'I can,' said Greeny. 'You're out.'

It was as if he had slammed a chair over my head.

'Wha? What do you mean, "out"?' I cried.

'As manager,' said Greeny. 'You're finished.'

My face burned fiery red with a mixture of fury, confusion, and bowel-loosening misery.

'But . . . but why?'

'Firstly, you and Natalie being together is no good for anyone,' said Greeny. 'We can't concentrate on getting better as a unit if you two are rowing all the time.'

'So why just me?' I said. 'Why aren't both of us out?'

'Well, Nat has really been doing most of the managing this year,' said Greeny. 'And she's been doing an excellent job.'

Natalie wouldn't take her eyes off the table top.

'Plus, there was the theft.' Greeny folded his hands together while my stomach twisted like an old rag.

'What theft? Y-you're talking out of your arse on this one, Green.'

'Then why are four Starfleet uniforms missing from my dad's costume store?' he said.

I gulped. 'Maybe he misplaced them?'

'OK. So why did you and Pete Cotterill turn up outside Natalie's house wearing them then?' he said. 'Whilst slapping each other?'

Harry and Ad gave each other 'What the cock has he done now?' looks.

'Look,' I said. 'That wasn't how it was supposed to—'

'Hey, I thought I might find you here.' I looked up and saw Pete Cotterill standing at the end of the table.

'You LITERALLY could not have picked a worse time,' I said.

« Older posts

'Shut up,' he said, jabbing at me with his finger. 'I want to know why you've been ignoring my phone calls. We had a deal, remember?'

'Oh God.'

'What deal is this, old son?' Harry asked.

Pete laughed. 'You mean you didn't even know about it? Why does that not surprise me? He told me that if I did that stupid Star Wars thing for him, I'd get to sing on one of your tracks.'

Everyone glared at me.

'It was actually **STAR TREK**, not **STAR WARS**,' I said, quietly.

Harry blew out through his lips and handed Pete a business card.

'Give me a call next week and we'll sort something out,' he said.

Pete nodded and gave me evils before leaving.

'Why did you tell him that, Joe?' said Greeny.

'I had my reasons,' I said. 'For one, you chumps would be lucky to have a world class vocalist like Pete on board, so . . .'

'It's all right, old boy, we know you've not been yourself lately,' said Harry. 'And that's why we think some time away from your managerial responsibilities would be best for everyone. You need to sort your head out and take care of yourself. Once you've done that, you can come back.'

'Can he?' said Greeny.

'Yes!' Harry fired back.

My stomach dropped. 'But my personal problems don't affect my ability to do my job.'

Harry quietly cleared his throat. 'You did book us to play a swingers party, old son.'

I slammed my hand on the table. 'How was I supposed to know what that meant? I thought they just really liked kids' play areas!'

'Ah, it weren't that bad,' said Ad. 'I got a free mask!'

'I'm sorry, Joe,' said Harry. 'We've made this decision because it is the best thing for you. You need less stress, not more.'

I looked across the table, unable to fully comprehend what was happening.

'I thought we were friends,' I croaked, which was every bit as pathetic as it sounds.

'We are, mate,' said Ad. 'We'll always be mates, you know that.'

'Real friends don't stab each other in the back,' I said.

'Joe—'

'No, Harry, don't try to sugar-coat your betrayal,' I said, my voice going all theatrical. 'I'm going, but I won't go quietly!'

I glanced around the table as I stood up. 'I'm going to take this . . . salt shaker. And there's nothing you can do!'

« Older posts

'I know, old bean, but it belongs to the cafe,' said Harry. 'It would be bad form if you took it.'

I sighed. 'You're right, it would be unfair on Mavis.' I scanned the table again.

'OK, well then, I'm going to take some of these chips, instead.'

'You're welcome to them, mate,' said Ad. 'I offered you some when you came in.'

'Um . . . good,' I said. 'Good. Because I'm really hungry so . . .'

I grabbed a handful and looked down at my betrayers. Natalie rested her head on Greeny's shoulder. It's funny how a small gesture can make you feel like your intestines are being forcibly removed with a rusty knife.

'It's been nice knowing you all,' I said, then turned around and walked out, hoping that stuffing chips into my face would stave off the tears at least until I got past the window.

It didn't.

Sunday 14th July
I am a broken man.

Monday 15th July
Broken.

Tuesday 16th July

Watched a few episodes of **DEEP SPACE NINE,** which was nice, but doesn't change the fact that I am broken.

Wednesday 17th July

'I'm broken, Troy,' I said. 'Totally broken.'

Troy took a long swig of his coffee. He looked like he hadn't slept.

'What's happened?' he asked.

'My friends have abandoned me,' I said. 'I am alone in the world.'

Admittedly, Harry and Ad had been trying to call me and even turned up at my house, but I didn't want them to see how they had BROKEN me.

Troy crossed his legs and picked at a loose bit of leather on his shoe. 'And how does that make you feel?'

'Are you not listening to me?' I said. 'Broken. I feel b-r-oken. And after we'd made that big breakthrough last week, too.'

'Right,' said Troy. 'What was it about again? **STAR WARS**?'

'**TREK**,' I snapped. 'Why can nobody ever get that right?'

Troy ran his hands down his face. 'Well, while I appreciate the progress we made with the doll last week, we're going to try something different this time.'

'That's a shame,' I said. 'I wanted to pretend the doll was

« Older posts

that idiot Greeny and throw it off a bridge.'

'Right,' said Troy, pouring himself another coffee. 'Well, on that subject—this week, we're going to try to deal with your obvious anger issues.'

'I do NOT have anger issues,' I barked, slapping a wicker basket of pot-pourri off the table.

Troy looked at the mess on the floor, then back at me. 'Some studies have suggested that transferring your anger to an inanimate source can help you stop taking it out on other people.'

'Oh my God, what are you talking about now?' I leaned back in my chair and stared at the ceiling.

'Well, you have spoken about your problems with saying the wrong thing and making rash decisions at times, particularly vis-à-vis Natalie, and this technique could help to prevent that from happening.'

I put all four chair legs back on the floor. 'OK, maybe it's worth a go.'

Troy grinned and threw me a pillow.

'That is the object that will take all your anger,' he said. 'Use it.'

I stared at the pillow, struggling to feel any malice towards it. To me, the pillow is a good thing—used for sleeping, burying your face in, and playful fights in those dreams about girls' slumber parties that I definitely don't still have on a weekly basis.

'I can't do it,' I said.

'OK,' said Troy. 'Well, what is making you angry right now?'

'Easy,' I said. 'It's the leavers' prom this weekend and I'm pretty sure Natalie is going with Greeny.'

'And are you angry about that?'

'Furious,' I replied.

'Good,' said Troy. 'Show the pillow.'

I growled and grabbed the pillow with both hands, as if I were strangling it.

'Natalie always hated proms,' I roared. 'She used to say they were stupid. Not so stupid now that skinny gym bunny wants to take her. I HATE YOU, GREENY!'

'Good,' said Troy. 'Let it all out.'

I punched the pillow until my fist went numb. The more I hit it, the clearer Greeny's face became.

'I REALLY HATE YOU!'

'This is excellent, Joe,' said Troy. 'Let the pillow take the punishment, so real people don't have to suffer. Then, maybe you could go to the prom.'

« Older posts

I stopped hitting and glared at him. 'Why would I want to do that?'

'It might be a good idea,' he said. 'Spending some time with other people might help get you out of your own head a little.'

'Yeah right,' I said.

'Please give it some thought,' said Troy. 'If you carry on like this and rid yourself of all that unnecessary rage, I bet you will be able to shake this Greeny by the hand with no problems.'

I threw the pillow to the ground and stamped on it seven times.

'Shake him by the hand?' I screamed. 'Not cocking likely!'

'OK, maybe we should start winding this up,' said Troy.

'NEVER!' I cried. I picked the pillow back up, spun around, and launched it at the wall with all my might. Of course, I have appalling aim, so it veered off course and flew out of an open window. It landed in the road and was run over by three lorries.

'Awww, that was my only anger pillow!' Troy moaned. 'I have another furious patient in this afternoon! I'll have to go to Dunelm!'

He slumped and grabbed his massive nose.

'Hey, if you don't like it, punch a pillow,' I said. 'Oh, that's right, you can't.'

You know what, I think this has really worked.

Thursday 18th July

Checked Greeny's Facebook.

My date's dress has arrived. Ain't she FIERCE? Im a luky guy ;)

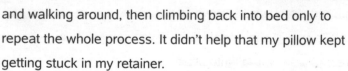

Underneath is a picture of Natalie looking beautiful in a tight-fitting black dress.

If anyone needs me, I'll be fighting every pillow I can find.

Friday 19th July

I hardly slept last night. I kept turning over and huffing—getting up and walking around, then climbing back into bed only to repeat the whole process. It didn't help that my pillow kept getting stuck in my retainer.

I was about to get up again when a massive head lowered itself into my field of vision.

'Move again and I will break your face,' it said.

'Someone's touchy,' I said.

Gav flopped back down on his bunk, making the whole thing groan. 'What's the matter with you, anyway?' he said. 'Still thinking about Natalie?'

« Older posts

I mumbled a 'Yes.'

Gav blew out through his nose like a bull. 'Between you and me, blud, I think she's being well harsh.'

'You reckon?' I said.

'Yeah,' he said. 'I mean, you kissed someone else? Big deal.'

I stared at my glow-in-the-dark stars on the ceiling. Some of them were peeling off.

'All the others hate me now, you know,' I said. 'They've sacked me as their manager.'

Gav tutted. 'Well, I ain't too surprised about that. 'You ain't exactly been hands-on, innit?'

I thought about arguing but decided against it. I picked up my phone—two fifteen.

'The way I see it,' said Gav, 'if you can get Nat back, the rest of them will fall into place.'

I laughed softly. 'Any ideas how I do that?'

'Nah,' said Gav. 'Don't ask me about girls. I'm a single man.'

'Are you?' I said.

He went quiet. I could hear Jim gently snoring next door.

'Yeah,' said Gav. 'Course I am.'

7.30 p.m.

I was thinking about what Gav said last night about trying
one last time to get Natalie back. The trouble with that
was, I had completely run out of ideas. In the end, I decided to google it. Sure enough, the ever-reliable **Men's
Domain** had an article on that very subject, titled **'Second
Chance Saloon—How to Win Her Back.'**

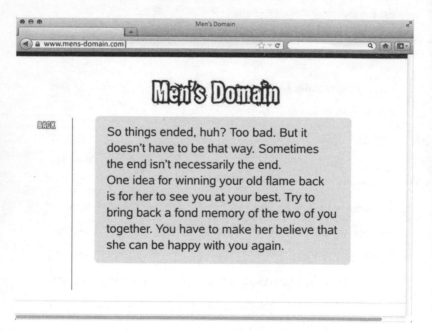

So things ended, huh? Too bad. But it
doesn't have to be that way. Sometimes
the end isn't necessarily the end.
One idea for winning your old flame back
is for her to see you at your best. Try to
bring back a fond memory of the two of you
together. You have to make her believe that
she can be happy with you again.

Thinking about it—this is perfect! Tomorrow night is the first
prom since the Easter one where we got together. I am
going to transport her back to that magical evening in what
will become known down the ages as the ultimate Grand
Gesture.

« Older posts

YES, CINDERELLA, YOU SHALL GO TO THE BALL!

Saturday 20th July

Just got back from visiting Doris. I asked her 'man friend',
the Colonel, if he had any advice for me on how to win
Natalie back. I thought it wouldn't hurt to get a bit of olden
days charm to back up my Grand Gesture. Let her into the
air raid shelter first, that kind of thing.

'Anyway, he said, 'tell her she's beautiful. And never
underestimate the power of a cheeky wink.'

To be honest, I thought he said something else at the
end there, and I nearly spat out my tea.

Right, blog. I'm ready to go now. Wish me luck!

12 a.m.

Did you wish it? I bet you didn't. Even though you're not
even a sentient being, I'm having doubts about your loyal-
ties.

Right. I might as well tell you what happened at the
prom, because I'm not going to get any sleep tonight, and
you've got nothing better to do.

I arrived fashionably late, my throat sore from rehearsing for my Grand Gesture. The SOUND EXPERIENCE were
already up, and everyone was on the dance floor. I noticed
Greeny wasn't doing his projections. No, because that
would distract him from HOLDING THE LOVE OF MY LIFE

AROUND THE WAIST AND DANCING WITH HER.

I went straight over to the buffet and crushed a handful of crisps between my fingers. That's you, Greeny, I thought. These Wotsits are you.

I couldn't allow myself to become too consumed with hatred, though. I had to concentrate. Blowing another Grand Gesture would be disastrous.

'Hey.' Someone shoved me in the back. I turned around to see Jamal Chauhan, Darren Ward, and Jordan Foster standing there.

'What do you want?' I said.

'We've just spoke to that pipe kid and he said he knew nothing about us being on one of their tracks,' said Jamal.

I dusted the Wotsit crumbs off my hands. 'Knock knock,' I said.

'What?' said Jordan.

'Knock knock.'

Jamal huffed. 'Who's there?'

'Arthur.'

'Arthur who?'

'Arthur Job.'

They stared at me like I was mental.

'Who the hell's Arthur Job?' said Darren.

I sighed. 'It means half a job. Maybe I should try it again in a cockney accent. Knock knock.'

'What are you on about, you tit?' Jordan shoved me again.

'You didn't hold up your end of the deal,' I said. 'And you have yet to return my VISOR, Jamal.'

'Yeah, well we were chased off by that mental PE teacher, weren't we?' said Jordan.

'Speaking of which . . .'

They beat a hasty retreat as Boocock stalked over.

'I didn't think you'd show your face here, Cowley,' he said, smoothing down his stupid moustache with his one good hand.

'I won't be intimidated by you, Boocock,' I said, trying not to make it obvious that I was SUPER intimidated. 'There are loads of witnesses here, and anyway, how do you know I'm not qualified in a martial art, like karate or feng shui?'

He blew out a load of air. 'I stand to lose my job because of you, you little worm.'

'What, as a PE teacher? Well, I must say, it's about time.'

'No, not as a teacher,' he said. 'As a PCSO. I've been accused of harassing a gang of **STAR TREK** kids.'

'Nothing to do with me,' I said, all innocent. 'You were

probably reported by an anonymous member of the public.'

He punched the ball of his palm, then winced slightly. 'I'm really gunning for you now, Cowley. Just you wait. I'll track you down—stalk you day and night until I can get you alone, then POW! I'll crush you like a COCKROACH.'

He held his fist right in front of my face. It shook with fury.

'Excellent,' I said. 'Now if you'll excuse me.'

I walked shakily away and looked up at the stage. I don't think Harry and Ad even knew I was there. Unbelievable. They'd be nothing if it weren't for me. I came up with that gay gimmick. And I'm the voice behind their big hit. Without me, they'll be playing old folks' homes again within a month.

I sat down on my own and observed my surroundings. Greeny and Natalie were still dancing, but I'd seen no evidence of kissing yet. If that happened, I'd go all Carrie on everyone's arses.

I wondered why Gav wasn't there. His overalls were drying on the line earlier so I knew he wasn't at work. It must be that mystery girl. Thing is, pretty much every girl in our year was accounted for at the prom. Maybe he's secretly taking ballet classes or something?

« Older posts

When the song finished, Natalie and Greeny stopped dancing and went to walk back to their table. Natalie saw me and froze for a second. Then Greeny pulled her in another direction and they sat as far away from me as they could.

I couldn't believe this. Last year when she'd see me, she'd break into this massive smile. Now it was like she'd spotted a Romulan or something.

You need to get this Grand Gesture kick started, my man, said Hank. *Before it's too late and she goes home with Slimmer of the Freakin' Year.*

I glanced over at their table. Greeny was holding Natalie's face close and saying something. She stroked his hand and looked at him with her big, sad eyes.

God damn it, do it now! Hank hammered coordinates into the console. *Go, go, go!*

I got up and marched over to the stage while my heart gave my ribcage some serious GBH. I knew this could be humiliating, but it didn't matter. I was never going to see most of these people again, anyway.

I couldn't let this go wrong like my last Grand Gesture. I had to keep it simple, but with the same impact. I unbuttoned my shirt so my **STAR TREK** tee was visible underneath and climbed the stairs.

'GREETINGS, OLD SON!' Harry yelled.

Ad grinned and clapped me on the shoulder. I could tell they were just trying to get back into my good books after stabbing me so ruthlessly in the back.

'I KNOW YOU DON'T WANT ME TO BE YOUR MANAGER ANY MORE, BUT I NEED YOU TO DO ME ONE LAST FAVOUR!' I screamed back.

Harry put his pipe back in his pocket and nodded. 'Of course.'

I passed him a USB stick with the karaoke version of 'Us Against the Universe' loaded on.

Harry turned the music off and everyone looked at the stage.

'What's happening?'

'Where have the tunes gone?'

A murmur began to ripple around the room.

'Hey, it's Puke!'

'He must be doing the song!'

A cheer went up followed by a 'Gay as the Day Is Long' chant.

'NO!' I yelled back at them. 'That's not what I'm singing. I'm doing a different song.'

The chant got louder, drowning me out.

I looked out at Natalie and Greeny and had a thought.

« Older posts

Maybe this could actually be a good plan. To show her than I can be a team player and that I deserve to be part of the SOUND EXPERIENCE again. A completely unselfish act.

'All right,' I yelled. '"Gay as the Day Is Long" it is.'

Ad passed me a mic while Harry started the track up.

This wasn't what we agreed, man! Hank screamed. *This is not part of the freakin' plan!*

'I'M AS GAY AS THE DAY IS LONG!'

A huge cheer went up and everyone started dancing. Every time I shouted the line, they all joined in. I felt like a rock star. I even threw in a few dance moves. I thought if I was going out, I might as well go out in style.

'I'M!'

'AS!'

'GAY!'

'AS!'

'THE!'

'DAY!'

'IS!'

'LONG!'

Another cheer shook the ceiling as the song ended. I stood on the lip of the stage, my arms outstretched, covered in sweat.

'Thank you, everyone,' I said. 'I'd like to dedicate that to Natalie. Natalie, I love—'

I stopped. Somehow, with all the thrashing around I was doing, I had missed the ENORMOUS COCKING NEWS CREW ON THE DANCE FLOOR. I didn't care about embarrassing myself in front of my stupid school year, but not the whole country.

'Oh, Christ on a penny-bloody-farthing!' I jumped off the stage and ran to the back of the room. Before I left, I stopped by Natalie.

'How was that?' I said.

She shrugged. 'Bizarre,' she said. 'But good on you for doing it, I suppose.'

'Well, that's me, I'm a team player,' I said. 'So . . . do you want to come for a walk with me or something?'

She pushed her fringe out of her eyes. 'No I don't, Joe.'

My heart shrivelled like a prune. 'But . . . why?'

'So what, you thought if you went up on stage and made an idiot of yourself, I'd get back together with you? As if it would make what you did OK?'

She eyeballed Lisa standing on the other side of the room. Lisa noticed her looking and stuck her tongue out.

'And you said some horrible, unforgivable things to me the other day. What were you thinking?'

'I don't know,' I said. 'I don't know what to do.'

'Don't do anything,' she said. 'Just . . . just leave me alone. For good.'

Greeny put his arm around her while I swallowed a

« Older posts

throat-lump the size of a bowling ball.

'Fine,' I said. 'But good luck teaching this idiot Klingon.'

She looked at the floor.

'Look after her, OK?' I said to Greeny. 'Treat her well.'

'Better than you ever did,' he said.

A low rumble of fury began to emanate from deep within my brain.

'I should have left you as a loner,' I snarled. 'Thinking of you as a friend was the worst mistake I ever made.'

'The worst mistake you ever made was kissing that skank,' he said. 'You're a nasty piece of work, Joe, and you don't deserve to breathe the same air as Natalie.'

Walk away, Joe, said Norman. *Don't let him antagonize—*

Before Norman could even finish his sentence, I'd already swung for Greeny, missed, and got punched to the ground.

'Greeny!' Natalie cried as she tried to help me up.

'No, leave me alone,' I said. 'For good.'

I got up and ran outside. My nose throbbed and blood ran off my chin onto my best Picard tee, but it was nothing compared to the pain of knowing that I'd lost Natalie forever.

1 a.m.

Gav has just sneaked back into the house. He smells like

my Steve Saint Laurence. Whatever. I don't need it any more.

Monday 22nd July

Mum came in and woke me up this morning.

'Whu-what do you want? It's seven o'clock.'

'You have to get up, Joe,' she said. 'You were in bed all day yesterday.'

'Yeah well, I'm still tired.'

Mum huffed. 'Come on. Up. I need to talk to you.'

I turned over and squeezed my zombie. 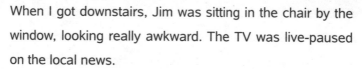 'We can talk later.'

Gav moaned and unleashed a fart that was like a clap of thunder over my head.

'Fine,' I said. 'I'm coming.'

When I got downstairs, Jim was sitting in the chair by the window, looking really awkward. The TV was live-paused on the local news.

'Morning, Joe,' he said over the top of his newspaper.

I unattached my retainer and plonked myself down on the settee. I planned on going straight back to bed after this and staying there for the rest of my life.

Mum walked in, chewing her nails. The baby monitor crackled into life and one of the babies started crying. Jim jumped out of the chair.

'I'll see to her,' he said, as he disappeared from the room quicker than a pube down a plughole.

'What's going on?' I moaned.

Mum pressed play.

'And finally, it was a very special leavers' prom at Tammerstone's Woodlet High on Saturday night, when top-ten dance chart hitmakers the *SOUND EXPERIENCE* played a triumphant homecoming set. Gabriel Bowen reports.'

This is bad, said Hank. *This is very bad. Look, I know this is going to sound whacked out, but try it. Concentrate really hard on the TV and maybe you can use your previously undiscovered telekinetic powers to cut the electricity.*

I stared. Nothing happened.

'The *SOUND EXPERIENCE*—who made their name as the only gay DJ duo in the country—are celebrating leaving Woodlet High in Tammerstone by playing a special gig for their fellow students.'

Come on, telekinesis!

The camera cut to the stage, where I was strutting around with an open shirt screaming, 'I'm as gay as the day is long!' over and over again.

I put my head in my hands. 'Oh my God.' Mum knew Harry and Ad had sampled me for the song, but she didn't know I was actually going to perform it live or anything. Neither did I, to be honest.

She paused the TV and sat down next to me.

'It's OK, Joe,' she said. 'It doesn't matter to me what your orientation is.'

I groaned and tried to convince myself that I was still in bed and this was all a nightmare.

Mum rubbed my back. 'Is this why you split up with Natalie? Do you talk about this with your therapist? You can confide in me—I'm your mother.'

'First of all, he's not a therapist, he's a counsellor,' I said. 'And secondly, I'm definitely not gay. We split up for . . . other reasons.'

Mum grumbled under her breath and switched the TV off. I'm glad she did. It was paused on a very unflattering angle of me.

'Can I go back to bed now?' I said.

'No,' she said. 'You've spent enough time there. And what's the matter with you, anyway? Is the therapy not working? Do you want me to make you an appointment with Dr Chang? See about putting you on pills? And what happened to your face? Where did that bruise come from? Why were you singing about being gay if you're not?'

'What is this, twenty cocking questions?' I said. 'I got the bruise when I fell out of bed, OK?'

Mum looked at me sideways. 'So why did you split up with Natalie then? What's the big secret? It's been the best part of a year now. Tell me.'

I rubbed my face. I'd avoided telling her for so long, but it would only be a matter of time before she found out. She's old, I thought. She'll understand.

'I, um, I kissed Lisa.'

'YOU. DID. WHAT?'

OK, maybe she won't.

'It was the worst mistake of my life, Mum. Please just leave it.'

'Oh, Joe, I thought I'd raised you better than that,' she said.

'Apparently not.'

She gasped. 'All this time I thought you were like me, but it turns out you're just like your father. Oh, poor Natalie. I bet that's why she hasn't RSVP'd our wedding invite.'

I stood up. 'She's over me, Mum. Got someone else. Don't worry about her.'

On the way out, I found Jim standing in the hall, rocking Ivy in his arms.

'It's OK, Joe,' he whispered. 'If you can't have fun when you're young, when can you, eh?'

I shrugged.

'Just do me a favour and don't tell your mother I said that.'

8 p.m.

Spent the whole day fielding phone calls from family.

Nan and Granddad Arnold: 'Well, it's a shock, but Larry Grayson was one of them and he was all right.'

Uncle Johnny: 'As a tribute to your bravery, dear nephew, I have moved two male dummies into the same box.'

Great-Auntie Teresa: 'I'll pray for your soul.'

Granddad Cowley: 'I was barking up the wrong tree buying you those Cojones magazine calendars, wasn't I?'

Had a text from Natalie:

I will forget it. That's exactly what I'm going to do. I am never going to think about her ever again. Ever.

12 a.m.
Can't stop thinking about her.

12.35 a.m.
Still can't stop thinking about her.

1 a.m.
Stopped thinking about her while I cut myself a slice of cheese. During that time I mostly thought about cheese. Then, once I'd swallowed the cheese, it was back to Natalie.

2 a.m.
The twins are crying. Think I might join them.

Wednesday 24th July
'I saw you on the news,' said Troy after a two minute silence. 'How does it feel to be famous?'

I picked at a loose thread on my jeans. I didn't feel like talking about the constant cycle of misery that is my existence.

'It's good that you have a creative outlet,' he said. 'I like making music, too.'

I sighed deeply and stared at the top corner of the wall. It was kind of dusty. I wondered how long it had been since it was cleaned. Probably years.

'So,' said Troy, 'is there anything you'd like to discuss?'

I shook my head.

'Well, then we'll move on to the prepared activity,' he said. 'What we're going to do today is a bit more positive than what we've done before. We're going to write a list of reasons to be thankful.'

I groaned. 'Well, at least it won't take a long time.'

Troy stood up and trudged over to the whiteboard. 'Come on, Joe, there has to be something.'

'Nope,' I said. 'I have absolutely nothing to be happy about. My life is a nuclear disaster.'

Troy gulped. 'OK, well, you're alive, right? Surely you can be thankful for that?'

I huffed. 'If you say so.'

Troy wrote 'alive' on the board. His hand seemed to be shaking.

ALIVE

'Um, you have somewhere to live?' he said.

'Yes, and it's a dump,' I replied. 'It smells of baby poo and I spend all my time alone because Mum and Jim are always planning their wedding and Gav is never in because he's having secret meetings with a mystery woman and sometimes I think I'd be better off living in a soggy cardboard box up an alley.'

'Well, surely you have something to look forward to?' said Troy, starting to look desperate. 'Why don't you organize something you will enjoy for a couple of weeks' time? Build up a sense of anticipation.'

'If it's all the same to you, I'd appreciate it if you kept your advice to yourself,' I said. 'You told me to go to the prom last week and look what that got me—a smashed-up face and indestructible footage of me parading around on the news pretending to be gay.'

Troy shook his head and sat back down in his chair. 'How could I have foreseen that happening?'

'That school is cursed,' I said. 'No good can ever come from me going back there.'

Troy gave me a patronizing little chuckle. 'I'm sure it isn't cursed.'

I picked up a plastic brain from the desk and tossed it up and down in my hand.

'Did you go to school, Troy?' I asked.

'For the last time, I did not forge my qualifications,' he said.

'No, I mean, do you remember what kids at school are like?'

Troy swallowed hard. 'Um, yes?'

'So then you'll realize why I didn't want to go in the first place,' I said. 'Everyone I ever went to school with is an idiot.'

Troy sat back down. 'Everyone? That seems unlikely.'

I laughed. 'You would say that. I bet you were never bullied. You were probably Mr Popularity.'

'I wouldn't say so,' he replied, taking a sip of his coffee.

'Oh no?' I said. 'So you're saying the other kids gave you a hard time?'

'Perhaps,' he said, shifting uncomfortably in his seat. 'But we don't need to talk about—'

'No, come on, let's hear it,' I said. 'What did they call you? Big Nose? Camel Face? Pinocchio?'

Troy touched the end of his nose and his bottom lip started to quiver. Then he leapt out of his chair and yelled, 'NO WONDER YOU'RE ALONE!' before storming out of the room.

To be honest, I feel kind of bad now.

Thursday 25th July

I was lying on my bed counting my teeth with my tongue when my door opened. Greeny.

'Who let you in here?' I said, still wondering why I had different quantities of teeth every time I counted.

'Your mum,' he said. 'I think she's worried about you, man.'

'No she isn't,' I said. 'No one cares about me.'

« Older posts

Greeny shifted awkwardly. 'Look, I ain't here to be your Antigone aunty,' he said. 'I just wanted to say I'm sorry.'

'What for?' I sat up too quick and whacked my head on Gav's bunk.

'Are you all right?' asked the winner of the World's Stupidest Question Championship.

I held my throbbing forehead and blinked back tears, partly from the pain and partly from the realization that the last time I did that, I was with Natalie. 'I'm fine,' I lied. 'Now tell me what you're sorry for. Punching me? Stealing the love of my life? You're going to have to be more specific.'

The impact from the head blow seemed to have broken one of the arms on my retainer and it hung off the side of my face like a wonky antenna.

'I'm sorry for hitting you,' said Greeny. 'You don't know how bad I've been feeling about that.'

'Not as bad as I have,' I said. 'But I'm surprised you're not even slightly remorseful about taking Natalie from me.'

'Look, man, I didn't take her from you,' he said. 'It's your fault you split up, and anyway—'

'I've heard enough.' I stood up and held my door open. 'I never want to speak to you again. Stay out of my way at *BUZZFEST.*'

Greeny's eyes went all watery. He stepped close to me. 'That thing on your face,' he said.

'It's called a RETAINER,' I huffed. 'And it's broken, thanks to you.'

He sighed gently and reached up to my cheek. I flinched, thinking he was going to hit me again, but instead, he grabbed the loose arm and fitted it back into the hole on the back of the headgear. He then leaned in closer and tightened the screw. When he'd finished, he stepped back and looked at me with his head cocked to one side, as if I were that knackered old camera from his kitchen counter.

'Good as new,' he said with a smile.

'Whatever.'

'Look, I just wanted you to know how sorry I am for hitting you,' he said. 'The way you've been acting is well out of order, but violence isn't my style.'

I turned my back on him. 'Fine. You know where the door is.'

I heard him start walking away and then stop. 'Just leave Natalie alone, OK?' he said. 'She's had enough.'

« Older posts

'OUT!' I yelled, waking one of the twins up and making them scream.

To think I was ever stupid enough to call him my friend. Well guess what? I don't need him. Or Natalie. You know, in a weird way, I'm looking forward to *BUZZFEST* now— spending it with my real friends.

7.30 p.m.

Oh damn it all to hell.

I've just got back from Harry's. I thought it would be a good idea to finalize all the details. Even though I wasn't their manager any more, I was still planning on going to *BUZZFEST* with them.

'Um, I'm afraid there's been a problem, old boy.'

'What now?'

'Well, I went to get my big tent out of the garage and it turns out mice have eaten bits of it,' he said. 'So I'm going to have to use the two-man one from the loft.' He screwed and unscrewed his pipe.

'And that is a problem why?' I said.

'Well, it means you don't have a tent, old son,' he said.

'Hold on just one fart-wafting second,' I said. 'How come I'm the one without a tent? What about Ad?'

'Well, we're the *SOUND EXPERIENCE*,' he said. 'We're sup- posed to be a couple, aren't we?'

I slapped the wall. 'I know what this is really about,' I said. 'It's the next phase of Operation Condemn Joe to a Life of Solitude and Misery.'

'Don't be stupid, old bean.'

'I thought singing that embarrassing song would have earned me at least some respect.'

'It has—you can still hang around with us,' he said.

'Oh, can I?' I said. 'Well thank you very much, YOUR BLOODY MAJESTY, but I think I'd rather spend time with people who actually want to be with me. THANK YOU VERY MUCH.'

He tried to stop me, but I stomped downstairs and out of the door. It would have been a better exit if his mum hadn't called me back and given me some fairy cakes to take home for the family, but you can't have everything. To be fair, they were pretty tasty.

I can't believe my own friends don't want to spend *BUZZFEST* with me. After how long we'd been planning for it as well.

You know what? I don't need them. I can have a perfectly good time hanging around with Gav.

11 p.m.

I will be forever alone.

When Gav finally got home, I asked him what he wanted to do at *BUZZFEST*.

« Older posts

'Ah, yeah.' He scratched the back of his head. 'I've been meaning to speak to you about that.'

'Oh God, you've sold your bloody ticket, haven't you?' I said. 'I knew you would. What was it for this time? Trainers? Some kind of special bouncy trainers? Well they'd better bounce you into the cocking stratosphere, matey, because I am most displeased about this.'

'What are you on about, you freak?' he said. 'I'm still going.'

'So what's the problem then?'

He puffed his cheeks out. 'I ain't staying in the VIP area, that's all. I'm going to hang on my own.'

I flicked my Lieutenant Worf Bobble Head figurine and watched his big, ridgy noggin wobble. 'So, what you're saying is, you'd rather go and camp in pleb class by yourself than spend time with your soon-to-be stepbrother in VIP?'

Gav looked around the room—everywhere but at me.

'Yeah, that's what I'm saying.'

I contemplated selling my ticket. I reckon I could get about five hundred quid for it. I mean what's the point in going when no one wants me to be there?

I'll tell you what the point is: spite. I've wanted to go to *BUZZFEST* since the dawn of time and nothing is going to stop me. I'm going to go on my own and have the best time ever. In fact, I'm going to take tons of selfies of me living it up, big style. Then they'll see that I don't need them.

Friday 26th July

All this do-it-alone stuff is fine, but I still need a tent. I don't own one, and Gav is taking his to the normal campsite.

Not that I'd ever contemplate sharing a tent with him, anyway. Unless I fancy dying of methane poisoning.

I asked Mum if I could borrow some money to buy some camping stuff. She refused, and said words that made my spine turn into candyfloss.

'Your Uncle Johnny has a tent you can borrow.'

Before I could scream, she was already calling him. Oh, how in the name of Satan's angry nipples am I going to get out of this one?

2 p.m.

Right. I'm standing outside his house writing this on my phone. I'm just going in, grabbing the tent, and getting the hell out of there. Five minutes, tops.

4 p.m.

Oh God. The smell is clinging to my clothes. I don't think I'm ever going to get it off me. The whole house stinks of dust and grime and loneliness.

Uncle Johnny lives on his own. Well, besides his collection of three hundred ventriloquist dummies. They take up every available bit of space—on shelves, on the back of chairs, hanging on the walls. All the while they stare at you with their dead, dead eyes.

'Greetings, Joseph!' Uncle Johnny shouted at me from the doorstep. His ginger mullet looked like it hadn't been washed since his jeans and denim jacket combo had last been considered fashionable. 'I heard from your mater that you require the loan of a recreational yurt for a weekend of harmonious revelries.'

'Um, what?'

'You want to borrow my tent.' He grinned at me with his weird orange teeth.

'Oh right. Yes please.'

'Good, then come in, my boy.'

He stood aside and let me in. The musty odour whooshed up my nose and almost made me gag. I tried to avoid looking directly at any of the dummies, but I could still feel their haunted eyes burning into me from every corner.

'I can't stay,' I blurted out.

'Why not?' Uncle Johnny frowned, his eyebrows like fuzzy ginger centipedes.

'I have to go . . .' My brain frantically searched for a decent excuse. 'To the doctor's.'

Uncle Johnny gasped. 'Nothing serious is it?'

'No,' I said. 'Just the runs.'

Nice, said Hank.

'You don't need to go to the doctor's,' said Uncle Johnny.

'Don't I?' I thought he'd rumbled me.

'No,' he said. 'Not when we have Dr Habooboo here to see you!'

He yanked a dummy in a white coat off a shelf and shoved it in my face. He then put on a show with it that lasted thirty-two minutes exactly. I have never been so freaked out in all my days. The entire time, I just focused on his Status Quo 1979 World Tour T-shirt, trying to figure out what had caused the large stain on it. I sincerely hoped it was toothpaste, but judging by the state of his teeth, it seemed unlikely.

Anyway, I managed to get the tent, that's the main thing.

So now I'm definitely going to *BUZZFEST*.

Alone.

Oh God, I'm going to end up like Uncle Johnny aren't I?

Sunday 28th July

You know, I think Sundays are scientifically longer than every other day of the week. I know it's twenty-four hours, but each of those hours seems to last five times as long. This might have something to do with the fact that I have to spend them at Dad's.

To begin with, he kept asking questions about Mum's wedding—whether she and Jim were still happy and stuff like that. I don't know why he suddenly cares now. If he had been this bothered about Mum's happiness when they were married they'd never have split up. When he realized I wasn't going to give him any answers on that score, he moved on to *BUZZFEST* and tried to verse me in festival etiquette. It was horrible.

'What festival have you ever been to?' I said.

'Glasto, 1994. It was epic. Saw the Levellers.'

'The who?'

'No, the Levellers,' he said. 'Anyway, dawg, I'mma give you the down-low, because you need to be wise if you want to have a good time, ya dig?'

I glanced at Svetlana, who was filing her nails with such ferocity that I'm surprised she had any fingers left.

I then had to sit there and listen to Dad's festival tips. He even wrote them all on his iPad and printed them off for me. I know, I'm ridiculously lucky.

Dad's festival tips

1. Stick with your homies. Pffft. I don't have any, so I can safely ignore that.

2. If anyone offers you drugs, just say no. Some playas just don't have the head for the herb. I don't know what any of that means, but I'm definitely not going to do drugs. I still need dissolvable children's aspirin for crying out loud.

3. Take plenty of toilet paper. Yes. And maybe I can use it to construct a bog roll friend.

4. Hide your valuables while you sleep. Wedge my phone in my bum crack. Got it.

5. Be safe. If you know what I mean.

'Yes, I know what you mean,' I said. 'I know exactly what you mean so don't say anything else.'

'No, what I'm trying to say is, have you still got enough . . . supplies?' he said. ''Cause if you've run out, I got your re-up.'

I'm going out for a while, said Hank.

Get back here, Hank, said Norman. *This is a two-man job, damn it.*

'Yes, I still have a full complement,' I said. 'So can we change the subject now, please?'

'Woah, woah, woah.' Dad held his hands up. 'You mean

HANK

NORMAN

« Older posts

you haven't used any of the condoms I gave you?'

'Well, I used one,' I said.

'Oh yeah?' he said. 'Well, one's better than nothing, I suppose.'

'Not really,' I said. 'I filled it with mayo and lobbed it at Gav.'

Dad shook his head. 'You want me to give you some tips for the ladies then?'

I glanced at Svetlana, scowling like a bulldog with haemorrhoids. 'No thanks.'

Monday 29th July

More wedding preparation happening. Mum has been on the phone to the Abbey where they're getting married. The Abbey is an ancient church that doesn't even have a roof. I asked why they didn't just get hitched down the tip and save a few quid, but apparently, that was me being 'grumpy'. Also, their reception is going to be in the function room at Woodlet High. I'm never going to escape that place, am I?

God, I am dreading this wedding. I mean, I've just about come to terms with the idea of being Gav's stepbrother, but the prospect of spending a whole day with my extended family is about as enticing as wiping my bum with sandpaper.

I keep checking my phone to see if Natalie has texted

but she hasn't.

NOT THAT I CARE.

Tuesday 30th July

'That's it, mister,' said Mum, opening the curtains at the crack of cocking dawn. 'You're getting a haircut. Today.'

I moaned and hid my face under my pillow.

'I told you, I'm not having a haircut until Natalie takes me back,' I said.

Mum wrenched the pillow off my face. 'Well you'd better watch out because one of these days you're going to wake up looking like bloody Hagrid.'

I gasped.

'Aw man,' Gav groaned. 'That's well harsh.'

Mum gave her forehead a one-handed massage. 'Look, son,' she said, 'it is my wedding soon. It is going to be the happiest day of my life and a new beginning for us all. I don't want you to look back at the photos in years to come and be embarrassed.'

'I won't be,' I said, shielding my eyes from the burning light.

'Trust me, you will,' said Mum. 'When I married your father, I had the biggest bubble perm you've ever seen. I looked like whatshisface out of Queen. Ooh, that rhymes.'

« Older posts

I turned over and rubbed at the sweaty bit under my retainer strap. 'I'm not getting my hair cut. If you're so ashamed of me, I won't be on any of the photos—how does that sound?'

Mum sat on the edge of my bunk.

'I'll give you fifty quid.'

Actually, this haircut might prove to be the fresh start I need. When I go to *BUZZFEST* alone, I will carve out a new identity as a cool haircut guy. I will meet other cool haircut people and hang out with them at places where everyone has a cool haircut and we will talk about how cool our hair looks.

I've googled 'cool haircut' and found one I think will really help with my transition. The **Men's Domain** hair expert calls it the 'Trident'. It's shaved at the back and sides, with the remaining hair swept forward into three large spikes.

Of course, the best place to get this done would be that fancy place, Lars Dulphgren's, but a cut there would set me back forty quid. That's practically all my money. I could just as easily go to Roger's Barbers, pay a fiver and have forty-five left to spend at *BUZZFEST*. Yep, this is the easiest decision I have ever made.

5 p.m.

What have I done?

I should have realized that it was a bad idea when I first walked into the shop. Roger took one look at me and nearly choked on his cigarette.

'Bladdy hell, kid, I thought you were dead,' he yelled. 'What happened to your hair?'

I shrugged. 'Felt like growing it. I need a cut now though.'

Roger nodded and gestured for me to sit down. 'I can see that,' he said, somehow stuffing a sheet into my collar, lowering the seat, and lighting another fag at the same time. 'This is going to be a bugger of a job.' He leaned towards a beaded doorway at the back. 'Pauline, cancel all my appointments.'

'What appointments?' was the reply.

He took out his biggest pair of scissors and started snipping.

'Woah, woah, woah.' I held up my hand. 'What are you doing? You didn't ask how I wanted it cut.'

Roger eyeballed me through the mirror as if I'd asked him to trim my bum fluff.

'But you have a short back and sides,' he said. 'You always have a short back and sides.'

'Not this time.' I reached into my pocket and pulled out my printout of the Trident. 'I want this.'

Roger pulled his glasses down from his forehead and squinted at the picture. A long stick of ash fell off the end of his cigarette and landed on my neck.

'That's not a short back and sides,' he said. 'That's . . . an abomination.'

'Well, so is that,' I said, nodding at a cobweb-riddled black-and-white poster of a cross-eyed bloke with a bowl-cut.

Roger shook his head. 'I don't know if I can do this, kid.'

'You can,' I said. 'Unless you're trying to tell me that—' I stopped and squinted at a framed certificate on the wall—'Big Steve's Saturday Snip Skool gives out qualifications willy-nilly.'

Roger puffed on his tab with a trembling hand. 'You're bladdy right,' he said. 'I am a qualified hair stylist. It's time to style some hair.'

I don't know why I didn't run. I suppose I thought that because Roger has cut my hair since I was a toddler, he would be able to do anything. I was dead wrong.

'Well,' said Roger, grimacing like he was being given a bikini wax by a gorilla. 'What do you think?'

He opened another pack of fags. I had been in the chair for an hour.

I looked at myself in the mirror. My hair was cropped short at the back, but he hadn't left enough at the front for some proper spikes, so I just had these matchstick-sized tufts of hair sticking up. This was not a Trident. It was more like a Spork.

'I look ridiculous!' I cried.

'That's what I've been trying to tell you!' said Roger.

'If you'd cut it like it is in the photo, it would be fine,' I yelled. 'Now pick some of my hair up off the floor and stick it back on!'

Roger dropped his bald bonce into his hands. 'Why couldn't you have had the short back and sides? It's the only cut anybody needs!'

I threw my hands up, sending millions of loose hairs flying into my own face. 'Fine. Do me a short back and sides.'

Roger blew a plume of smoke at the yellow-stained ceil-

« Older posts

ing. 'It's too late for that,' he said, his voice cracking. 'It's too late.'

So now I have a number one all over. I look like a cocking thug! Gav likes it, but he would because it is the exact same haircut he has. And he doesn't even have to pay for his—he gets my mum to shave his head over the sink.

OH MY GOD. There's no way I'm going to be able to hang out with cool haircut people now. The only gang I'm going to be able to join is a racist prison one.

The worst of it is, I'm not even one of those people who look good bald. My head is all weird and bumpy. I look like a Klingon crossed with a hard-boiled egg.

'It's OK, Joe,' said Mum. 'It'll grow back.' Then she turned to Jim. 'I've changed my mind, you're wearing hats for the wedding.'

'But you said—' Jim interjected.

'YOU'RE WEARING HATS,' said Mum.

Wednesday 31st July

'I see you've had a haircut,' said Troy. 'Good. Perhaps this is a sign of your moving on to a healthier outlook?'

I shrugged and fiddled with a bust of this beardy bloke called Freud that was on the desk. I was cooking up some kind of joke to do with the fact that his name sounded like 'fraud' but I couldn't quite manage it.

'Look, Joe,' said Troy, leaning forward and resting his

elbows on his thighs. 'I would like to apologize for last week. I acted unprofessionally and that was unacceptable.'

I gulped and stared at the grim brown carpet tiles.

'Yeah, me too,' I said. 'I shouldn't have pointed out your massive nose.'

Troy nodded briskly and smiled. 'OK,' he said. 'Now let's work through your issues. I promise not to make you do anything gimmicky this time. We'll just talk. Tell me what's on your mind.'

I took a deep breath. 'Well, where do I start? I've been scalped by the world's worst barber, I'm pretty sure my dad is having some sort of mental breakdown and I'm going to *BUZZFEST* this weekend all alone. Some shady character is bound to take me under his wing and turn me into his drug mule.'

'Wait a second.' Troy held up his hand. 'You're going to *BUZZFEST*?'

'Yes,' I said. 'And after that, I'll probably be caught halfway to Nicaragua with a dozen johnnies full of ching chang charlie in my stomach. Why do you ask?'

'No reason,' he said. 'Please, go on.'

'Well, I think I might be overthinking it with the whole drug mule thing, but I'm still going to be careful, and will probably avoid people with names like "Sound Pete" or "Brickface". I know they say you should be open-minded but—'

'Are you sure it's a good idea?' Troy interrupted me.

'What, drug muling?'

'No,' he said. 'Going to *BUZZFEST*. I just think it might be a bit much for you—all the noise and stimulation could cause you to lose your equilibrium.'

I looked at him. His upper lip was sweating and his leg was shaking.

'What's your angle, Troy?' I said, narrowing my eyes at him. 'Are you after my ticket or something?'

'Oh, don't be so ridiculous,' he said. 'I'm just thinking about your well-being, that's all.'

He wouldn't look me in the eye.

'No dice, Troy,' I said. 'You're up to something. What is it?'

Troy blinked hard. 'In all my time as a counsellor, I've—' He stopped himself. 'Sorry, I was about to be unprofessional again.'

I stood up and started pacing in front of him. '"In all my time" you say? Seems an interesting turn of phrase. Normally people would say "in all my years". How long have you been in this job exactly?'

'Sit down, Joe,' said Troy. 'This is irrelevant.'

'Never!' I yelled. 'Now spill it—how long have you been here? In fact—' I lunged at his certificate. 'You have blanked out the date on this thing. And not even very well—you've just stuck a bit of masking tape on the glass.'

'Get away from that!' He leapt to his feet and tried to stop me, but I'd already unmasked his deception.

'Two months?' I shrieked. 'You've only been qualified for two months?'

'Calm down, Joe,' he said.

'Calm down?' I cried. 'Calm down? I'm entrusting my mental health to the care of a work experience boy! I bet you're the same age as me!'

Troy ripped some pens out of his shirt pocket and threw them to the floor. 'I'll have you know I am twenty-two years old and have been told I'm VERY MATURE FOR MY AGE!'

'Just because you wear a cardigan doesn't mean you're mature!' I yelled.

'Does, too!' he screamed back.

'Does not.'

'Does times a trillion.' Troy stamped his feet.

'DOESN'T TIMES INFINITY!'

'DOES TIMES INFINITY TIMES INFINITY.'

'YOU CAN'T TIMES INFINITY BY INFINITY.'

'YES YOU CAN!'

'NO YOU CAN'T.'

'YES YOU—' Troy stopped and held the bridge of his nose. 'I can't do this,' he said, quieter. 'I'm going to have to ask you to leave, Joe.'

'Go on then,' I said.

Troy grabbed a handful of his own hair. 'Leave, please.'

'OK.' I turned and headed for the door.

« Older posts

'And I think it would be a good idea if you saw a different therapist after *BUZZFEST*,' he said as I left.

'That sentence is only accurate if you remove the word "different",' I fired back, before slamming the door behind me.

7 p.m.

OK, maybe I didn't say that last bit. I might have mumbled, 'Whatever,' then tried to slam the door but couldn't because it had a soft-close mechanism.

Thursday 1st August

BUZZFEST tomorrow. I have:

One tent.

One sleeping bag.

One hypoallergenic pillow.

One bag of clothes.

One night-time retainer.

Two pairs of wellies. (One for daytime and one for night. The night ones have hi-vis stripes.)

One stuffed zombie. Shut up—if it gets cold, I might need to cuddle something for warmth.

One tub of sandwiches. Two cheese, two ham, one jam (pudding).

One large bottle of water.

Two packs of wet wipes.

Three *STAR TREK* annuals.

My phone. I should really take that picture of me and Natalie off as my background. I'll get around to it one day.

Friday 2nd August

BUZZFEST

It's scary here. When we saw it on the horizon—a sea of tents and stalls and stages—my stomach flipped. I had been dreaming of this moment for years, but the closer we got to the entrance, the more frightened I became.

'This takes me back,' said Jim as he weaved in and

« Older posts

out of groups of people lugging camping stuff. 'Back in the nineties, me and Chips used to go to all-night raves in places like this.'

Gav looked at him as if he'd just admitted to being a Pokemon. 'You were a raver?'

Jim nodded. 'Big time.'

'Well what happened?' said Gav.

Jim chuckled and gave him a sideways look. 'You did.'

Jim dropped us off at the entrance after warning us not to do any of the stuff he used to do back in the olden days. The first thing we saw after we got our wristbands was a bloke on stilts in a jester's hat.

'Welcome to another woooooorld, boooys,' he yelled.

I had to hold Gav back from knocking him over, which was hard when I was carrying half a cocking campsite on my back.

The whole place smells odd, like a mixture of straw, mud, and this weird, sweet smoke. A man in a leather gimp suit strolled past and no one looked twice. It was terrifying. I didn't really want to walk to the VIP area by myself.

'Are you sure you don't want to come with me?' I said to Gav.

'Yeah,' he said. 'I told you, I'm chilling by myself, innit?' He kept shifting

from side to side. Seeing him standing there in his tracksuit and fake Burberry cap amongst all that madness was like seeing a rhino in a library. Like, ridiculously out of place.

'Well, can I just wait with you for a while?' I said. 'I'm a bit tired.'

His mouth went all tight. 'Nah,' he said. 'You better get going.'

'But . . .'

He gave me a look—one of those deadly ones he used to give me at school when he was about to dunk me through a basketball hoop.

'Fine, I'm going,' I said, and scurried away as fast as the ten ton weight I was heaving would allow.

Why is he being so weird, anyway?

By the time I got to the VIP area, I had seen the following things:

- Two girls mud-fighting.
- Three pirates breakdancing.
- A clown on a quad bike.

It really is another world. To be honest, I'm not sure I like it.

Luckily, as soon as I flashed my fancy red wristband to security, I found that the VIP campsite has a bit of a different feel to the main one. There is more space, nicer looking toilets, and even electric hook-ups so you can charge your phone.

I went to pitch my tent in a quiet corner, but this bloke in a trilby said he'd already reserved that spot. I said I didn't think you could do that, but he just kept nodding and sniffing, so I moved. It was then that I found Harry and Ad's tent. Completely by accident. I wasn't looking for them. Not at all.

'What the Dickens happened to your hair?' said Harry.

'Hello, mate!' said Ad. 'It's wicked that you found us.'

'Yeah, right,' I said as I threw all my crap on the floor.

Thing is, this was the first time I'd ever pitched a tent. I'd only ever been camping once before and that was a disaster. I was six and got stung by a bee, so I threw a wobbly until Dad sprung for the hire of a static caravan. Anyway, it was just a bit of canvas and some poles. How hard could it be?

Turns out very cocking hard. I refused all offers of help and somehow managed to zip myself inside it and get stuck. I'm still not sure how that happened. That was when I heard voices. Them.

'Is that Joe?' said Natalie.

'Um, yes,' Harry replied.

'Oh God, I thought he wasn't hanging out with us.'

'I can hear you, you know,' I said from my sweaty canvas prison.

'Do you want me to give you a hand with that, Joe?' said Greeny.

'You mean you want to STEAL my tent?' I said.

'What?'

'Well, you've stolen everything else of mine.'

Natalie growled. 'We are not doing this again.'

I pointed in the direction where I thought she might have been standing.

'I know we're not,' I said. 'We've been dreaming of coming to *BUZZFEST* for years, and now we're finally here we're going to have fun. Barrels of it, baby!'

'Well, I think we'll leave you to have your barrels by yourself,' she said. 'Come on, Greeny.'

'No, we shouldn't let him ruin it,' said the stupid knobber.

'I know, but if I stay here, I'm going to be miserable,' she said, as a small piece of my soul shrivelled and died.

'Fine,' I said. 'Leave. I'm going to have soooo much more fun without you. Not just barrels, but, like, canisters. Giant oil canisters of fun.'

'They've already gone, old son,' said Harry.

'I'm well aware of that.'

Sweat ran down my back and into my pants.

'Do you want me to unzip you, Joe?' said Ad.

'Yes please, Ad.'

I grudgingly allowed them to help me put my tent up. It looks kind of pathetic compared to all the hoity-toity VIP tents that are probably en-suite and have their own butler to wipe your bum for you.

'Now we've just got to put the waterproof cover on, old boy,' said Harry.

He opened the bag and spread it on the floor. It was only then that the true horror revealed itself. Uncle Johnny had had it customized.

'Oh for cocking out loud, I can't put that on!' I said.

'I know,' said Ad. 'I mean, your name ain't even Johnny so you might forget it's yours.'

I buried my face in my hands.

'If you don't put it on, you'll get soaked, old son,' said Harry.

'I'd rather be wet than single myself out as a complete freak.'

Harry chuckled. 'You do that well enough by yourself.'

I smiled even though I didn't want to.

'Come on, old boy, you might as well hang around with us,' he said. 'If you think about it, this is how it was always supposed to be. Just the three of us.'

I scratched the back of my bristly head and stared at the floor. 'I suppose you're right,' I said.

'Of course I am,' he said. 'We're going to have the best time ever.'

I looked over at the other side of the field and saw Natalie and Greeny putting a tent up. Tent in the singular. They're sharing a tent. They. Are. Sharing. A. Tent. I need to take my mind off this right now.

11 p.m.

The bands don't start until tomorrow so there wasn't really much to do other than sit around playing Would You Rather?

For a while, we had a gap next to us which had been saved for those other two people who shall remain nameless called Natalie and Greeny, but then three girls turned up and started pitching their tents there. Harry and Ad hopped around like a couple of excitable gibbons at feeding time.

'A blonde, a brunette, and a redhead,' Harry giggled. 'One of each!'

I didn't even look because I have given up girls. I view them only as vaguely interesting members of a different species. I am like David Attenborough watching toads.

When they'd finally got their tents up, two of them came over to us.

'Thanks for your help, by the way, guys,' said the redhead.

'Yeah, not very chivalrous, are you?' said the brunette.

'That's where you're wrong, ladies,' said Harry, taking his best pipe out. 'I am so chivalrous that, if we were walking

together, I would lay Ad's coat in a puddle so you wouldn't have to walk through it. Besides, we would never assume that you couldn't assemble a tent by yourselves. We are not the unreconstructed chauvinists we may appear.'

They laughed and introduced

themselves. The red-haired one was called Verity and the brunette was Jasmeen. Harry was just about to launch into one of his lectures about how only real men smoke pipes when Verity stopped him, frowning. 'Wait a minute, don't I know you from somewhere?'

'I don't know,' said Harry. 'Did you perchance watch the Mr Universe pageant this year? Modesty forbids revealing the result, but let's just say the crown fits perfectly.'

He winked at me. I just carried on tearing up grass.

'No, that's not it,' she said. 'Where have we seen them before?'

'I don't know.' The brunette leaned behind the tent. 'Hey, Mila, come here a sec.'

The blonde one who I now knew to be called Mila emerged from inside. She's quite nice-looking if you're into that sort of thing. Which I'm not.

'Where do we know these guys from?'

Mila cocked her head to one side and squinted at us. 'Oh gosh,' she said in an accent I couldn't quite place. 'It's those gay guys!'

Harry's face fell like a house of cards built on a cobweb.

'Oh yeah!' said Verity. 'THE SOUND EXPERIENCE!'

Then they started singing 'I'm as Gay as the Day Is Long'.

Harry facepalmed.

'We should totally hang out with them,' said Jasmeen. 'I mean, it's not as if they're going to try to take advantage of us, is it?'

'No, of course not,' said Harry, punching the side of his tent.

'Yeah, you can defo hang with us,' said Ad. 'We're as day as the gay is long.'

After a while, they all decided they were going to get burgers for lunch. The problem with that plan was that the burger place was in the main part of the site, out of VIP. Eek. No thanks. I said I'd stay put because I had some ham sandwiches, but Mila grabbed me by the hand and dragged me.

Once the others had bought their food, we all sat on the floor in a circle, not far from a bloke who was chanting poetry into a bucket. While they all talked and got to know each other, I kept checking my phone. For no reason. I wasn't expecting Natalie to get in touch or anything like that.

'Who's that? She's pretty.'

Mila pointed at the picture of Natalie on my background.

'She's a girl I used to see,' I said. 'We were in love.'

She frowned. 'But . . . I thought you were gay.'

The conversation in the circle stopped.

'What, you mean you're not?' said Verity.

'I'm not, no,' I said. 'I'm just their ex-manager.'

'But Harry says you were the one who said, "I'm as gay as the day is long",' said Jasmeen.

'I was a very dedicated manager.'

Harry looked like he wanted to die. I could read his mind: *How are you getting out of this gay thing without us?*

I knew he wanted to tell them the secret, but if he did, it would jeopardize the 𝒮OUND EXPERIENCE'𝒮 existence. Imagine if it got out that they were straight. It would totally wreck their career.

'So, what happened?' said Mila when the conversation returned to normal. 'I mean, with the girl?'

I blew out and rubbed my chin. 'Um . . .'

'I'm sorry.' She held her hands up. 'That was rude of me. I'm always too, how do you say it in English? Nosish?'

'Nosey,' I said. 'And it's OK. We split up because I made a mistake. I kind of kissed another girl.'

'Ah.' She smiled sadly. 'And you're sorry?'

'I've never been sorrier,' I said.

We didn't say anything for a while. I scanned the field for Natalie but I couldn't see her. I tried to stop my brain imagining her and Greeny in that tent together, but I couldn't do it. I needed a distraction.

'I have an ex, too,' said Mila. 'I'm glad I'm away from him. Looking back, I don't why we were ever together. He could be nasty at times and we had nothing in common. He made fun of me because I liked Pink Floyd.'

I nearly choked on my ham sandwich. 'Y-you like the Floyd?'

'Of course I do,' she said, grinning. 'Who doesn't like them?'

I gestured at the others. 'What do you lot think of Pink Floyd?'

Ad blew a raspberry, Harry made an 'I'm totally hanging myself' gesture and I'm pretty sure one of the girls called me 'Granddad'.

'See?' I said.

'Ah, they don't know what they're talking about,' said Mila. 'Hey.' She leaned close and whispered in my ear. 'Want to see something cool?'

'Um, yeah, I suppose.'

Her eyes darted around. I noticed for the first time how big they are—her eyes I mean. And they're grey, too. She

« Older posts

looks like a manga character.

'This is how much I love the Floyd,'
she said, then super quick pulled the neck
of her T-shirt down and showed me what
was, quite unmistakably, the prism from
The Dark Side of the Moon tattooed on
the Top Side of Her Boob. Then, just as
quickly as she had pulled it down, she
yanked it back up.

'Wuh-huh,' I spluttered. 'How very . . . fetching.'

You're a smooth guy, Cowley, said Hank. *A regular
James freakin' Bond.*

Mila laughed hard. 'You're blushing!'

I felt my cheek. It was hotter than Ad's arse must have
been after he sat on a barbeque for a bet.

'Yeah, but this is just sunburn,' I said. 'I don't have as
much hair as I used to.'

Mila laughed so much she had tears in her eyes. 'But it
is cloudy!'

Then I started laughing too. I couldn't help it. 'Where did
you say you were from again?' I asked.

'The Netherlands,' she replied.

I nodded. 'Wow, the Dutch really are more liberal than
us.'

'Not my dad.' Mila wiped her wet cheeks. 'He would freak
if he saw my tattoo. Luckily, he still lives back in Amsterdam

so I don't see him that much.'

I gasped. 'So you're from a broken home too?'

Mila looked confused. 'No, my house is fine.'

Yeah, I suppose that British saying didn't make it to Holland.

'So, um, what are you doing in England?' I asked. 'Business or pleasure?'

Ah, so that's how you talk to girls, said Hank, slapping Norman on the back. *Act like a freakin' customs official.*

'My family have just moved here,' said Mila. 'My mother and the other girls' fathers work together for PGS Records. The Amsterdam office has merged with the London one.'

Ah, so that's why Harry is so keen to stick with these girls. He's trying to schmooze a record deal. I glanced over at them. I noticed Ad's eyes lingering too long on Jasmeen's cleavage and gave him a quick kick on the shin. He forgets that those glasses magnify his eyes to such a degree that it is obvious what he is staring at. And it won't do for a gay DJ to be eyeballing boobies.

'You must really like the Floyd to get them inked on your body for the rest of your life,' I said to Mila.

'They're the best,' she said. 'I will always love them. You should get one too.'

I laughed. 'I don't think I'd ever be that brave. Plus, the tattoo shops near me are kind of rough. This one place is called Crazy Dave's. I'm sorry, but I refuse to let someone who calls himself "Crazy" anywhere near me with a sharp needle.'

Mila giggled and hit me on the arm. 'You are funny, Joe. In my country, we would call you a grappenmaker.'

'A crappenmaker?' I said. 'As in someone who is full of crap?' I stopped and shrugged. 'I've been called worse.'

'No, grappenmaker,' she said. 'It means someone who makes jokes.'

For Christ's sake, kid, Hank interrupted. *Do not use this as a platform for all your lame STAR TREK gags.*

I concur, said Norman.

'Oh, thanks.'

Mila balled up her cardboard burger tray and fired it towards a bin, missing by miles. 'So did you like my tattoo?' she asked with a smile. 'You seemed a little shocked.'

'Y-yeah, it's great,' I said. 'I've just never been flashed like that before.'

Mila laughed again and patted my knee. 'Well, you're a Floyd fan so I knew you'd appreciate it. Would you like another look?'

'Um . . .'

Before I could figure out how to say yes without sounding like a huge perv, she pulled her shirt down and showed me again.

'Look at the detail on the light beam here,' she said,

pointing with her little finger. 'It took a while to get right but it was worth it, don't you think?'

Oh my God, she is wearing a red bra. It has a little bow on the front. I think there's some lace on the side . . .

Why are you concentrating on the bra, idiot? Hank yelled. *Who are you, Ann freakin' Summers?*

'Yeah, it's brilliant,' I said. 'Where you did you, um . . . get it done?'

Mila pulled her shirt back up. 'My friend Emma did it. It was sore to begin with but you get used to it.'

'You know tattoo artists?' I said. 'That's really cool. I mean, I like drawing but my friends aren't exactly very arty.'

I nodded across to Harry and Ad who were farting into bottles and sealing the lids 'for later'.

'You're an artist?' said Mila. 'Awesome. Hey, who knows? Maybe you can draw my next tattoo?'

I spluttered. 'What, actually on you?'

Mila laughed again. 'You are a grappenmaker, Joe.'

I'm lying in my sleeping bag now. I wish I'd brought an inflatable mattress or something because no matter what position I lie in, there is always a huge clod of earth prodding me in the spine. I need to sleep but the idea of Natalie and Greeny in a tent together keeps going round and round in my mind like a carousel designed by Beelzebub himself.

It's going to be a long night.

« Older posts

Saturday 3rd August
3.45 a.m.

I woke up in the night with a bladder like
an overinflated balloon. If I'd stayed asleep
two minutes longer, there would have been a
genuine pee emergency and that tent would
have become uninhabitable. I rubbed the gunk
from my eyes and stared at my glow-in-the-dark
Enterprise watch. Three o'clock. Ugh. Why couldn't it wait
until a reasonable time? How old am I, ninety?

I knew there were toilets on the other side of the food
vans, but that was a five minute walk. I considered going
up the nearby fence but this was a VIP area and they might
have me kicked out. There was no alternative. I would have
to trek to the bogs.

I unzipped the tent and shivered as a cold wind blew in
and rattled the sides. I pulled on my hoodie and got out.
Everything was quiet in my area, but there were campfires
dotted about with people still sitting around them.

I walked on, tripping over stupid guy ropes every three
steps. Turns out the stringy street lamps were about as
much use as a sparkler in a black hole.

After I'd finally reached the toilets and drained my explo-
sive wee bag, I decided to take a different route back. The
fact that this route would take in the site of Natalie and
Greeny's tent had absolutely nothing to do with it. I just

wanted a change of scenery. At three in the morning.

I roughly remembered where it was and crept in that direction. It was all quiet. That was a good thing. At least I think it was—I still can't make up my mind. I was sure I could hear Natalie breathing as she slept. I remembered it from when she used to fall asleep on my bunk. Not because I was boring but because, I don't know, maybe my mattress was really comfy.

Anyway, I decided to move on before I could be rumbled and headed to the nearest path. There was a big campfire up ahead with four people sitting around it on what looked like rocking chairs. Weird. I kept my head down and hurried on, silently panicking that I wouldn't be able to find my tent until daybreak.

'Heyyy, not so fast!'

I ignored the shout from the campfire and carried on.

'Woah, little dude, he was talking to you.'

I stopped and turned around. Everyone around the campfire started laughing.

'Awesome headgear,' one of them said.

Ah crap. I had somehow forgotten about the retainer. I was so used to wearing it that I didn't stop to consider that it might look weird in public. Still, they didn't exactly have much room to laugh. They all looked ridiculous. This one bloke had a hair bun and another had a handlebar moustache. The fire made it shine as if it had been thoroughly waxed.

'Aw, leave him alone,' said the only girl, who was wearing a TUXEDO. 'I think he's on fleek.'

I was going to say thanks, but she said it in this way which might have been sarcastic. I had no idea. Plus, Jehosifer only knows what the cocking hell 'fleek' means. Is it some kind of drug I haven't heard of? I decided I would be better off saying nothing.

'He's not fleek, he's more like geek chic,' said Handlebar.

'Yeah, and geek chic is so last week,' slurred some idiot who was wearing a T-shirt with a cartoon of Hitler in a mankini on it.

I stood there, my face burning with rage and embarrassment, but my over-tired brain was unable to think of a decent comeback. 'Yeah well, I'm going now,' I mumbled.

'Oh no, no, no,' said Hairbun. 'We have to get a pic with you. You're too good to be true. I mean look at that **STAR TREK** hoodie!'

They all got up and started walking towards me.

'Oh yah, I'm putting it straight on my Instagram,' said Handlebar. 'Hashtag no filter.'

I rubbed my eyes and tried to figure out if they were speaking in code like really crap Russian spies.

'Instagram is for the masses,' Mankini Hitler spat. 'Everybody in the know is on Daguerreotype now. Uses the same effects as the earliest camera from 1839. Twenty minutes to take a photo. Don't you know anything?'

A look of horror passed across Handlebar's face. 'Yeah, of course I do,' he spluttered unconvincingly. 'I was just being ironic.' He forced a laugh. 'Hashtag check out my Myspace.'

I stepped back and nearly landed arse first in someone's tent. They had me surrounded.

'Just leave me alone,' I said. 'Or . . . or I'll get a guard.'

They all laughed and Tuxedo called me a 'darling little flower' in that same sarcastic voice she seemed to be stuck with permanently.

'Hold on, I'm going to get my selfie stick,' said Handlebar.

'Um, that's ironic too, right?' Mankini Hitler asked.

I could tell Handlebar literally wanted to kick Mankini Hitler in the face but couldn't because he was like his boss or something. 'Um . . . yes?'

'Correct answer,' said Hairbun. He then stole a quick look at Mankini Hitler. 'Isn't it?'

Mankini Hitler nodded and twirled his diamond-studded cane.

« Older posts

They stepped closer to me, their phones out, ready to snap some ironic-or-not-ironic-I-have-no-idea selfies with me. I held my hands up to my face. I could have just let them do it, but there was something nasty about this. I didn't like the idea of being a figure of fun on Daguerreotype, or whatever it was called. If my humiliating photos have to be online, I prefer to keep them confined to Facebook.

'Aww, come on, little buddy, you're so retro-fleek, you don't even know it,' said Tuxedo. 'You're like a postmodern work of art!'

This would never have happened if Roger had given me that cool haircut. They would have accepted me as one of their own!

One of them grabbed my hand and tried to force it down.

'Hey, Joe!'

I looked up the path and saw Mila walking towards us.

'What's going on?'

'We have to get a selfie with this little guy,' said Hairbun. 'I mean, just look at him, isn't he precious?'

Mila ignored him. 'Do you want your picture taken by these people, Joe?'

I shook my head.

'Then I ask that you let him go,' she said to them.

'Awww, you're no fun,' said Handlebar.

'Let him go,' Mila said, firmer this time.

The gang glanced at each other. 'What if we don't want

to?' said Mankini Hitler. 'You have to admit, a genuine retainer-wearing nerd is a real find.'

The others hooted their agreement.

Mila narrowed her eyes and folded her arms. 'What did you just call that?'

The cheering died down and Mankini Hitler gulped. 'Um, a retainer?'

Mila stifled a laugh behind her hand. 'Oh my God, I thought you guys were cool.'

They looked at each other nervously. 'W-we are?' said Handlebar.

'We are not,' Mankini Hitler snapped. 'We are post-cool.'

Mila winked at me and smiled. 'Well, if you are so post-cool then you will know that that installation on Jasper's face is not a retainer.'

Jasper?

There was silence. All you could hear was the crackling of the fire and the faint hum of their wind-up gramophone.

'Th-then what is it?' Handlebar asked.

Mila sniggered. 'If you have to ask, you're not in the know.'

The gang stepped away from me and burst into nervous, hysterical laughter. 'Of course we know what it is!' said Handlebar, rubbing his waxy tache frantically. 'I was just

« Older posts

kidding! It's a . . . you know, it's a . . . you tell them, Clementine, I have to sneeze.'

Tuxedo blinked hard. 'Yeah, of course I know what that is, I have one on order from Iceland. It's being polished by Eskimo artisans as we speak.'

'Yeah, mine too,' said Hairbun.

'Mine's being blessed in a sacred ceremony by Navajo Indians before being shipped across the Atlantic on a steamboat,' Mankini Hitler whimpered, seemingly on the verge of tears. 'I'M GOING TO BED NOW!'

Without another word, they all scampered into their respective yurts and wigwams. Mila giggled and grabbed my arm.

'What the hell was that?' I whispered to her as we walked away.

'The only way to deal with nasty hipsters is to prey on their biggest insecurity—being behind fashion.' She had this massive smile on her face as she huddled close to me to keep warm. 'There are so many people like that in Amsterdam. My ex was one.'

'Really?' I said. 'I can see why you hate him.'

'Totally,' she said. 'Once we had a fight when I told him his ear trumpet was stupid. He got so mad, he rode off on his unicycle.'

I laughed so hard I nearly tripped over yet another guy rope.

'Thanks for not making fun of my—' I pointed at my retainer.

'Oh, don't be silly,' she said. 'I think it's cool.'

I raised my eyebrows.

'I'm serious. And not even in an ironic way,' she said. 'I like the fact that you wear it in public without caring what people think. You're like the Anti-Hipster.'

'Um, actually, I just forgot I had it on.'

Mila laughed and dug me in the ribs with her spare hand. 'You are so funny, Joe. I had no idea going for a late night pee would be such an adventure.'

'Me neither,' I said.

'Anyway,' she said. 'Here is my tent, so . . .'

She let go of my arm and stood opposite me. I didn't know what I was supposed to do. Shake her hand? Salute?

Before I could move, she stood on her tiptoes and kissed my forehead. 'It was the only part I could get to,' she said. 'Night!'

'Night,' I replied, watching her disappear inside and wondering what this weird feeling in my stomach was.

10 a.m.

It must have rained after that and my lack of waterproof cover meant I woke up completely soaked. Excellent.

The smell of burning wood drifted in. The others had built a campfire and were sitting around it talking. They must have thought I couldn't hear them despite the fact that the tent is made of thin canvas and I was RIGHT NEXT TO THEM.

'He's been depressed about her dumping him for like nine months now,' said Ad. 'He keeps this toy she bought for him and takes it everywhere.'

'Ugh, that sounds well creepy,' said Verity.

'I think it's sad,' said Mila. 'Poor Joe.'

'He needs to snap out of it,' said Harry. 'Because she's not going to change her mind, and every time he tries to put it right, he makes it worse.'

But none of that was my fault. Bad stuff just happens to me. I know if I could just get through to her once, without Greeny or anyone else getting in my way, she would change her mind.

I realize I said I'm finished with girls now, but balls to it. I am going to get Natalie back and I'm going to do it this weekend.

What better place than *BUZZFEST* for a Grand Gesture?

I chucked my retainer in my bag, changed into some slightly less damp clothes and jumped out of my tent.

I spotted a glint of purple over by the breakfast van. I threw my wet wellies on and started running over. Mila stood up and stepped in front of me.

'Hey, Jasper the hipster, are you going to get breakfast?'

'Yes, no, maybe,' I said. 'I'll catch up with you later.' I carried on running, never taking my eyes off Natalie.

I dodged between tents, hurdling guy ropes like I was on course for Olympic gold. When I got to the van, Natalie was halfway along the queue.

'Hi,' I said.

'Hey, get to the back!' yelled the trilby bloke.

'It's OK, I don't want breakfast, I have perfectly good ham sandwiches,' I replied.

'What is it now, Joe?' Natalie folded her arms.

'I just want ten minutes of your time,' I said. 'That's all.'

'You had six months of my time and look where that got me,' she said.

« Older posts

I rubbed my eyes and tried to swallow the lump in my throat. 'It wasn't all bad, was it?'

'I'm just trying to get a bacon roll here.'

'Was it?' I said.

She sighed and kicked a paper cup away. 'OK, it wasn't all bad,' she said. 'But when you did what you did you ruined everything.'

'I know,' I said. 'But I just wanted to speak to you while we're here. Do you know how long it's been since we sat down and talked, just the two of us?'

She shrugged.

'So, will you meet me later?' I said. 'I promise I won't try to force you to get back together with me or anything like that. I just miss talking to you.'

She looked at me for the first time. 'Fine.'

I grinned like a moron. 'Great,' I said. 'So how about one o'clock?'

'No good,' said Natalie. 'I'm seeing the Buzzards then.'

'Two?'

'Nope. Chronic Tremor.'

'Three?'

'Murderblades.'

'Four?'

'OK,' she said. 'I'll meet you by the Ferris wheel at four. We will talk until ten past. Then you will leave me alone for the rest of the weekend. Deal?'

'Deal,' I said. 'And you won't bring Greeny?'

'If it means that much to you, I won't bring Greeny,' she said.

I went back for my breakfast sandwiches and pondered my next move. I have until four to come up with a Gesture Grand enough to win her back.

3 p.m.

'Her favourite TV show is **STAR TREK: THE NEXT GENERATION** and her favourite book is the first Lord of the Rings one,' I said. 'Oh, and her favourite colour is black.'

'Hmm, I can't think of anything,' said Mila. 'Maybe you could just try talking to her?'

'Trouble is, my talking skills are awful,' I said.

'I don't know, you've been doing OK with me,' she said.

We were standing right at the back of the Main Stage field. Some awful indie band called the Sadsacks were onstage, farting their way through a song called 'Emotion Sickness'.

'Yeah, but when I'm with Natalie, it's different,' I said. 'I really love her.'

Mila's smile dried up and she looked back at the stage. Must have been something I said. See? Talking isn't going to cut it.

'How about music?' she said, still not taking her eyes off the stage. 'I mean, I bet she doesn't like Pink Floyd, does she?'

'No,' I said. 'I did try but she couldn't get into them. Her favourite band is Oh, Inverted World. She is obsessed with them.'

Mila looked back at me and smiled. 'I may be able to help you.'

She grabbed my hand and dragged me through the crowd until we got to this menacing-looking bouncer by a gate.

'Hey, Lucius,' said Mila.

A big grin spread across the bouncer's boulder-face. 'Mila! How you doing?'

'Pretty good thanks,' she said. 'You look like you've lost weight.'

I hoped she was lying. Any bigger than he already was and he would have taken up all the mass in the known universe.

'You coming in?' he said.

'Yes please,' said Mila. 'And can I bring a plus-one?'

The bouncer looked me up and down and nodded.

Mila shouted her thanks, grabbed my hand and pulled me through the gate.

'Where are we going?' I said.

She laughed. 'It's a surprise!'

We were running through this weird area. It was like VIP, but even more VIPish. Instead of tents, there were trailers and caravans. And instead of sniffy blokes in trilbies, there were stressed-looking people in suits shouting into mobile phones.

We got to this caravan and she knocked on the door. After a couple of seconds, a scary-looking blue-haired bloke answered.

'Hey, Mila, how's it going? Come on in.'

He let us inside. I had no idea what was happening. For all I knew, she could have been taking me to be the sacrifice in some kind of satanic ritual. I mean, I hadn't even known her twenty-four cocking hours!

Once I surveyed my surroundings, I started to calm down. This place was way too nice for human sacrifice. Even though it was a caravan on the outside, it was nothing like one on the inside. There were fancy leather chairs, games consoles, plasma TVs, everything.

'God this is loads better than my nan's place at Rhyl,' is a sentence I still can't believe I said out loud.

The bloke who let us in chuckled. He looked familiar. As did the other three lounging around on settees.

'Joe, this is Lucan, Ralph, Zeggo, and Pog, but you may know them as Oh, Inverted World.'

Jesus of Nazareth at a roller derby!

'Your boyfriend a fan?' said Pog.

'No, no, I'm not her boyfriend,' I said. 'To be honest, we only met yesterday.'

'Yeah, we're just friends,' said Mila, digging me in the ribs.

'Well, any friend of Mila's is a friend of ours,' said Lucan, giving me a double thumbs up. God, these emo bands are more cheerful than their music would have you believe.

'I was hoping you'd say that,' said Mila. 'Because I have a favour to ask you.'

'Sure,' said Lucan.

'Could you guys sign a picture for Joe? He has a friend who'd really love it.'

'That it?' he said. 'I thought you were going to ask us to do another charity record. Don't get me wrong, I like to do my bit, but I got two kids in college.'

Anyway, they agreed to sign it and I left the caravan holding what could be the key to Natalie's heart.

'Thank you, thank you, thank you.' I hugged Mila tight. When I let her go, her face was all red. I must have squeezed too hard.

'It's OK.' She giggled and tucked her hair behind her ears. 'I'd do anything for my friends. We are . . . friends, aren't we, Joe?'

I looked at the photo, still amazed. 'Mila, if what you have done helps me get Natalie back, I will be your best friend forever.'

She patted me on the shoulder. 'So shall we go and hear some music?'

I checked my watch. 'OK, there's still plenty of time. Let's go.'

We went over to the Main Stage to watch the Jingle Jangles. Not my kind of thing, but Mila said they're one of her favourite bands—huge in Holland apparently. After what she did for me, I couldn't really refuse.

I wasn't paying attention to their set though. I was too busy thinking about how Natalie would react when she saw that signed photo.

To Natalie,
Thanks for being awesome,
Lucan, Pog, Zeggo, Ralph.
Oh, Inverted World.
PS: Make it so!

« Older posts

PERFECT!

I felt a hand grab mine.

'This one is my favourite!'

Mila swayed along to the music and made me do the same. After a while, she put her arm around me and her head on my shoulder. I didn't know what to do. 'I love these guys almost as much as the Floyd,' she said. 'Do you like them?'

I didn't want to say no so I said, 'Um, well, I'm sure they'll grow on me.'

'Hey,' she said when the song had finished. 'You told me you were an artist. Do you have some drawings I could see?'

'Um, not really, no,' I said.

'You mean to tell me you don't have any pictures on . . . this?' She reached into my pocket and grabbed my phone.

'Ah, come on, Mila, give it back,' I said.

She held the phone above her head. 'You'll have to come and get it.'

I reached for it but she backed away.

'Please,' I begged. 'I need it.'

Mila laughed and skipped away, nearly tripping over a comatose man dressed as a Teenage Mutant Ninja Turtle.

'Now the monkey comes out of the sleeve!' she yelled.

'What?' I cried, making another futile grab. 'That is the

weirdest thing I have ever heard and I've known Ad for a decade!'

'You don't have that phrase in England?' She clasped my phone in both hands and held it behind her back. I put my arms around her to get to it.

Mila laughed, her candyfloss breath tickling my face. 'OK, I'm sorry, Joe. You can have it back.'

A man in a thong just happened to be walking past, and in a moment of pure horror, she lifted the band and tucked my phone in there.

'NO!' I leapt forward and grabbed the phone, along with a decent portion of hairy man arse. He turned around. 'Ooh, hello,' he said. 'I'm flattered but I don't swing that way.' Then he carried on strolling around in obscene underwear as if it was the most normal thing on earth.

Mila bounced around like Tigger on crazy pills, laughing so much I thought she was going to pass out. I looked down at my hand. No matter how much I wash it, it will be forever tainted.

'You are really annoying, do you know that?' I yelled.

She stopped bouncing. And laughing. Her face went proper sad. I stepped towards her but she turned her back on me and sat on the floor. She pulled her knees up close to her body and rested her head on them.

« Older posts

Now you've done it, you goddam moron, said Hank. *You and your anger issues.*

I think you should apologize, said Norman.

I sat down next to Mila and awkwardly put my hand on her back. 'I'm, uh, sorry.'

'What for?' Mila didn't even turn and look at me.

'For saying you're annoying. I shouldn't have said that.'

Mila turned around and stared at me stone-faced. Her eyes seemed even bigger than before. My whole body was being squeezed by the ragged claws of Guilt. Mila seemed really cool and I hated the idea of upsetting her. Then she broke out into a massive smile. 'I got you, Joe!'

'What?'

Are all Dutch chicks this insane? said Hank.

'I got you to apologize even after I nearly shoved your phone up that man's zitvlak!'

She hooted and jabbed me. I tried not to laugh but I couldn't help it. It was infectious. I jabbed her back. Then she kicked things up a gear by tickling me.

Here's the thing, blog. I HATE tickling. It is the worst thing in the world. If I had been captured by the Cardassians instead of Captain Picard, all they'd have to do is brush me with a feather and I would be screaming 'There are five lights!' in milliseconds. I think it stems from when my mum tickled me when I was little and I laughed so much I puked in her perm.

I rolled on the floor to try to get away, but Mila was on me like an unstoppable tickling machine.

'Please!' I screamed. 'Stop!'

She carried on, pressing down harder.

'I'll wee myself!' I yelled.

'Fine,' she said, ceasing her brutal assault. 'I wouldn't want you to make your trousers even more damp.'

She reclined beside me, propping herself up on her elbow. 'Now are you going to show me your art or what?'

I fought to get my breath back. 'Fine,' I panted. I opened my phone's images and scrolled through until I got to my drawings folder. I tried not to think about where my phone had been and quickly passed it to Mila.

She started with a smile on her face, but the further she scrolled, the less happy she looked. I think I know why. When I first started saving my stuff on there, I was with Natalie, so I mainly drew nice things—but then when she dumped me, it got darker. Crows, coffins, self-portraits of future me working as a cleaner in KFC and making sleazy remarks to young girls who'd come in for a Krushem.

Mila locked my phone and passed it back. 'You're a really great artist, Joe,' she said.

'Oh,' I said, my face going all pink again. 'Thanks.'

'But there's a lot of sadness in you, isn't there?'

« Older posts

I shrugged. 'I don't know,' I said. 'I suppose there is. But then there are also ham sandwiches, so make of that what you will, and anyway, those were all works in progress. I'm planning on going back and making some of them a little less depressing.'

Mila squeezed my knee. 'No, I think you should draw what is in your heart. If it's sad, then that's OK. Here,' she said, reaching into her pocket and pulling out a pen. 'Draw me.'

I laughed a bit too loud. 'What? Here? Now? I've got nothing to draw you on.'

Mila looked around at the disgusting littered floor and found a reasonably clean cardboard burger tray. 'Here is your canvas.'

She sat up opposite me cross-legged, a look of peaceful anticipation on her face.

'OK, fine,' I said. 'But if I end up making you look ugly, it's not my fault. I'm used to working on, you know, actual paper.'

Mila smiled shyly and interlocked her fingers. 'So you're saying I'm not ugly?'

I gulped.

Proceed with caution, said Norman. *Consider every word before you say it.*

'Of. Course. You're. Not. Ugly,' I said.

For him, that's not bad, said Hank.

'Oh you charmer, Joe,' she said.

I looked at her as I sketched. I know I'm not exactly One Ear Van Gogh or one of those other lads but I like to think I have my own style. I noticed how the sun made her hair shine and her grey manga eyes glow. I tried my best to tune out all the distractions—the music, the shouting, the bloke puking into a novelty hat—and focus on getting Mila's essence onto the page. Or burger tray.

'OK,' I said after a while. 'It's done. If you hate it, please don't tickle me again.'

Mila scooched over to me and sat close, her bare leg touching my thigh.

'Ah, Joe,' she said. 'I love it.'

'Really?' I said.

'Yeah.' She traced a finger down the lines. 'You are great at drawing. You really have it under the knee.'

I looked at her sideways.

'Is that another Dutch idiom you don't get?'

I nodded.

'I'm going to have to learn some of your British sayings.' She picked up the drawing and held it up to the light. 'Hey, give me your phone again.'

I did as I was told and she took a photo of the burger

tray. 'Your drawings will get happier from now on,' she said. 'This one will remind you of the great time you had at *BUZZFEST* with your new friend Mila.'

I chuckled to myself. I suppose it would make a nice change from all the misery.

'I'm really touched by this,' Mila went on, carefully putting the drawing in her pocket. 'In fact, you might say I'm "over the moon". That is one of your British sayings, isn't it?'

I laughed. 'Yeah it is.'

'See, I'm learning quickly.' She looked straight at me. 'Thank you for this.'

There was this moment, then. I have no idea how long it lasted but we seemed to stare at each other for ages. It was weird and kind of awkward, but I didn't want to look away. I could feel us getting closer. It was kind of nice. Soft and fuzzy.

Suddenly, an icy finger of dread ran up my back. This couldn't happen. Whatever this was. I was supposed to be planning my Grand Gesture.

I shook my head and moved away slightly.

'Is everything OK?' Mila asked.

'Yeah, yeah, yeah, everything's fine,' I said, jumping to my feet. 'I just need to . . . go back to my tent. For a little while. Yes, that's it.'

Mila frowned, then smiled and nodded. 'OK.'

'Thanks for the . . .' I pointed at the signed photo.

'No problem,' she replied. 'Thank you for the portrait. Maybe sometime this weekend, I can draw you?'

I glanced at my watch. 'Um, yeah, absolutely. Maybe. We'll see . . . Bye, Mila.'

Without looking back, I walked away, back to the campsite. What the cack happened there?

I'll tell you what happened, said Hank. *For the first time in nine months, someone made you forget to be miserable about Natalie.*

Ah, Natalie. My one true love. She will never leave my synapses again.

Right, it's half three. Time to go.

The next time I come back to this stinking tent, my life will have changed for good, I know it.

6.10 p.m.

I've washed thoroughly several times and yet I still can't seem to shake the smell of poo. How did this happen? How did I get here? I need to piece together everything that took place.

I walked around the shopping area, past stall after stall filled with flags, wellies, and Rasta hats, looking at the signed picture and rehearsing what I was going to say to Natalie. I was going to tell her how I got the band to sign

« Older posts

it for her, to show how much I cared. I was convinced this Grand Gesture would be a success, because it wasn't too flashy or crazy. It was intimate and low-key. She would love it.

By the time I reached the food stalls, my stomach was groaning. I couldn't face the idea of eating though. Plus, six quid for a cup of noodles? When Gav, the Pot Noodle connoisseur, sees that, he'll flip.

I glanced at my watch. Five minutes to go. I hadn't strayed too far from the meeting point, so it didn't take me long to get there. Natalie hadn't arrived yet, but I tried not to worry too much. She wouldn't stand me up.

I pulled the picture out again and ran my hand over it. If this went well, I knew it could be the photo that changed my life.

I heard a voice shouting over the hum of distant music. I didn't pay any attention to begin with—the mentalists at this place shout all the time. But it kept going.

'OI!'

There was something familiar about it. And aggressive. Very aggressive.

'IS THAT YOU, COWLEY?'

I looked up and saw him charging through the crowd,

tossing people aside like Optimus Prime smashing through a woodshed.

He had a bandage on his arm and was wearing a blue polo shirt with 'EVENT SECURITY' emblazoned on it.

No. Surely not.

'B-B-BOOCOCK!'

I tried to run, but my crap wellies slipped in the mud like Scooby Doo when he sees a ghost. He got closer, but I just about managed to get some traction and make my escape.

'You can't do this, Boocock!' I yelled. 'I'm supposed to be meeting someone.'

'Oh, you'll be meeting someone all right,' he growled. 'Your maker!'

I ducked into a crowd leaving the arena and slipped through to the other side. Boocock was too big to get through.

'You can't hide, Cowley!' he screamed.

A wasted-looking guy stopped. 'Hey, man. You need to chill.'

Boocock didn't take too kindly to being told to 'chill' and, without a word, headbutted him to the ground.

Oh dear, said Norman, mashing the controls.

Jeez, if that's what he did to that slacker, imagine what he's going to do to Joe, said Hank. *Run, you freakin' moron!*

I sprinted past another throng and scraped through a gap between two burger vans. I wasn't looking where I was going and tripped over a cable, clattering to the ground like a bag of old spanners. Before I could move, Boocock had crashed through the crowd and was on top of me, breathing hot gusts of corned-beef-sandwich breath all over my face.

There was nothing else to do. I had to arm my secret weapon. The one that can only be used as a last resort.

Begging.

'Please, Mr Boocock, sir,' I whimpered. 'I'm sorry. I understand that you're angry but please don't hurt my face, I'm meeting a girl.'

Boocock's snarl turned into a wicked grin.

I realize it's a little late now, said Hank. *But you probably shouldn't have told him that.*

Boocock curled his hand into a fist. 'This one will be for when you broke my ribs.'

'But I didn't!' I said. 'Th-that was an accident.'

He drew his fist back. Then I had an idea.

'This one isn't though,' I said, and quick as Superman after eight cans of Red Bull, kneed him right in the knob.

He fell off me, howling in pain and screaming the kind of disgusting words you only normally hear on Gav's rap albums. I jumped to my feet and sprinted away, through the gap between the burger vans and into another food area. I thought I'd lost him, but he was up again, chasing me down.

'Jesus Christ, he's like the cocking Terminator,' I panted.

I weaved in and out of bodies and campfires and inflatable sheep. I didn't realize I was being chased into a dead end until it was too late. An immense barrier of Portaloos

blocked my path like a stinky Great Wall of China. There was only one thing for it.

I threw the toilet door open and jumped inside, bolting it before Boocock could reach me. Nothing could have prepared me for the smell. Why was this one so much worse than the VIP toilets? Do rich people's dumps smell sweeter or something? I gagged. It was truly awful. Like one of Gav's farts to the power of seventy-eight kajillion. I pulled my T-shirt over my nose and tried to hold my breath.

Boocock banged the door.

'You can't hide in there forever, Cowley!' he screamed.

'Yes I can!'

I took my phone out and tried to call either Natalie or the police. No service. Perfect.

'If you come out now, I promise I won't beat you too badly. Maybe I'll leave you with a couple of teeth.'

I held my breath as long as I could. When I felt myself beginning to lose consciousness I had to take a gulp of air. It was disgusting. I bet my lungs are now permanently coated in cack particles.

'GET OUT OF THERE, COWLEY, OR I WILL RIP THE DOOR OFF AND SMASH YOUR FACE IN WITH IT!'

Oh balls. Oh balls. What do I do?

I'm afraid I can't see a way out of this one, said Norman.

Listen, I know this might sound wacky, but have you considered squeezing out through the toilet? said Hank.

I honestly don't know why I bother. More bangs echoed off the walls, sending ripples through the disgusting sewage soup in the hole below.

'Hey!' I heard a different voice.

'What do you want?' said Boocock.

'I saw you chase that boy into there.' The voice sounded familiar. It was a girl. And kind of foreign.

'So what if you did?' said Boocock. 'Now, do one before I have you kicked out.'

'Leave him alone.' She sounded deadly serious. Wait a minute. Mila!

'Or what?'

'Or my mother, who is one of the main shareholders in this festival, will have you dismissed. Now go.'

I could actually hear Boocock breathing.

'You know what?' he boomed. 'You can STICK yer job.'

It went quiet for a second. I thought he might have gone. Then I heard the sound of straining. And I was pretty sure it wasn't someone in the next cubicle.

'Stop it!' Mila cried.

I didn't know what was happening. Until the front of the cubicle started to tilt backwards.

'No! NOOO!'

Before I could make a break for it, I was thrown against the wall as the whole revolting Turdis toppled over. I lay on my back, winded but still breathing. For a second, I was relieved.

I had escaped injury.

But then the flood happened.

Gallon after gallon of foul brown sludge gushing out of the hole, covering me from head to foot.

I wanted to scream, but some kind of survival instinct kicked in and I realized that to open my mouth would be literally the worst thing I could do.

I climbed to my feet, disturbing the slop and making the smell even worse. I managed to get the door open and hoist myself out. My cack-covered wellies slipped on the edge of the upturned crap house and I fell off the side onto the ground.

I don't know what was worse, the smell or the laughter. No, it was definitely the smell. Mila stood over me with her scarf over her mouth.

'Oh my God, Joe, are you OK?'

'Never been better,' I said.

'That terrible man is gone,' she said.

Panic shot up my back. 'Wait, what time is it?'

'It's ten minutes past four, but you can't . . .'

I jumped to my feet and ran back towards the meeting point, shedding clumps of soggy toilet paper with every step and fighting my body's overwhelming urge to vomit until my abdomen was completely hollow. Funnily enough, people got well out of my way.

When I got there, Natalie was about to leave.

'Natalie!' I yelled after her. 'Wait!'

« Older posts

She turned around, her face angry and hurt.

'I can explain!'

Her expression turned from upset to disgusted.

'Oh my God, Joe, are you covered in sh—'

'Yes,' I said. 'Yes I am. But that hasn't stopped me getting you this.'

I pulled the picture out of my back pocket and held it out to her.

'I am not touching that, Joe, it's caked in . . . Jesus, I think I'm going to be sick.'

I looked at it. Sure enough, all you could see was a couple of the blokes from Oh, Inverted World and a LOAD of poo.

'Is this some kind of stupid joke?' said Natalie from behind her hand. 'Because I don't find it funny.'

I facepalmed, which was horrible because my hand was slathered in crap.

'I'm going,' she said.

'But, Natalie . . .'

'All you had to do was turn up on time, talk for ten minutes, and leave, but you couldn't even do that,' said Natalie. 'Even by your standards, this is messed up.'

I went to protest but she was gone. I stood there, in the middle of the shopping area, alone, like some kind of pooey Bigfoot, while people on the Ferris wheel took aerial photos of me.

I ran straight to the VIP showers, but I wasn't allowed to use them because I was 'too dirty'.

Too dirty to use a shower. Yep. This is what my life has come to.

In the end, I found a big lake and flopped into it. I then abandoned my clothes and walked back to the tent in nothing but my soaking, see-through white pants. At least I was at *BUZZFEST* and didn't look out of place.

Anyway, whatever. I am never coming out of this tent. I am going to live in this field forever. People will talk of a wild man roaming the hills. Some will call me a demon, others an alien. I will become part of local folklore. Old men will gather their grandchildren around the fire and tell them never to wander into the hills alone. I will be dreaded but revered, until one fateful day when a farmer shoots me when he catches me trying to eat one of his sheep.

Gah. You know, for years I wanted to come to *BUZZFEST*, but like everything else, it has been nothing but a massive nut-bag-kicking disappointment.

« Older posts

12 a.m.

I must have fallen asleep after writing that last entry because the next thing I knew, someone had poked their head into my tent.

'Hey, it's Crapman!'

'Oh bum off, Harry,' I groaned, at least thankful that I'd had the presence of mind to get dressed after my eventual shower, emergency injection at the medical tent, and thorough wet-wipe wash. 'And anyway, is Crapman really the best you could come up with?'

'All right, how about, Crapman: the Dark Shite Rises?'

I turned over and stared at the sopping wet canvas centimetres from my face. 'Just leave me alone.'

'No can do, old boy,' he said. 'You have to vacate your tent and try to enjoy *BUZZFEST*.'

BUZZFEST can buzz off,' I said. 'I want to go home.'

'That's it, MOBILIZE TROOPS!'

Another four pairs of hands appeared and started yanking at my trouser legs. It was like something from Resident Evil.

'Fine. FINE. I'm coming.'

I climbed out of the tent and stretched. People nearby spluttered and nudged each other.

'I'm so sorry, Joe,' said Mila. 'I didn't want to tell them, but . . .'

'We made her!' said Verity. 'She was laughing so hard, we knew something was up.'

'Yeah, thanks, Jasmeen,' I said.

'I'm Verity,' she said.

I screwed my eyes shut. 'Sorry. I'm rubbish at remembering names.'

'He's bad at names but he's good at faeces,' said Harry.

Everyone laughed. Even Ad, and I can guarantee he didn't get it.

I gave Harry a two-finger salute.

'Hey, if you don't like it, you can sewer me,' he said.

I could tell it was going to be a long night.

We all went down to the arena to watch some bands. Harry had his arm around Verity and Ad was holding Jasmeen's hand. I stood there alternating between checking my phone and looking around for Natalie.

We ended up in the small Unsigned Artists tent because the girls wanted to watch this up-and-coming rapper their parents' record label was interested in. They made us go right down to the front.

'His name is MC Camelface,' Verity yelled over the warm-up music. 'There's been a lot of buzz about him lately and we want to make sure he doesn't go elsewhere.'

When he came on going, 'Yo, yo, yo, what's happenin', *BUZZFEST*?' I knew something wasn't right. There was something a little bit odd about him. And familiar. Very familiar.

'Aight, I'm gonna get to the stuff you know in a little bit, but first I'm gonna do a new track. See, I've recently been thinking about a subject very close to my heart: bullying. When I was at school, the other kids used to make fun of me cos of my big nose.'

Wait a minute.

The crowd started booing.

'Troy?' I yelled.

'But I stopped letting it get to me. I owned it. That's why I use the name MC Camelface. Recently though, as part of my job helping youngsters in the community, I met a young guy who brought all those bad feelings back, and he inspired me to write this.'

Straight away, the DJ played a heavy beat and the whole crowd started bouncing. I couldn't believe it. I mean, I remember him saying something about making music, but I thought he'd be part of a ukulele orchestra or something like that. Not this.

'I walked into school and all the kids froze,
They said, "Look at that freak with the big fat nose."
I used to sit in my room and cry and bawl,
Till one day I stood up and said, "F*** YOU ALL!"'

The crowd went wild as he launched into the chorus.

'I'm Camelface, standing tall and proud,
I'm Camelface, shouting it loud.
I'm Camelface, you'd better know.
I'm Camelface, so F*** you, Joe!'

'What?' I cried. 'This has to be a breach of patient-slash-whatever-you-are con-fidentiality!'

Troy looked right at me as he launched into the next verse. I could have sworn he winked.

Mila tugged on my arm. 'That is so funny—it's almost as if he's talking about you!'

I turned around and got out of there around about the time he got the whole tent to join in with the 'F*** you, Joe' bit. So that's why he didn't want me to go to *BUZZFEST*. It was nothing to do with my 'equilibrium'. He just didn't want me finding out he was a stupid rapper.

« <u>Older posts</u>

I met the others outside after he'd finished. All I could hear from the people flooding out of the tent was how amazing he was.

'He was SICK,' said Jasmeen, and I'm pretty sure she didn't mean that in a vomity way.

'I'm going to call my dad right now and tell him he has to sign him!' said Verity.

'No!' I yelled.

Everyone stared at me. 'Why not?' said Mila.

'B-because some of the people he raps about might take umbrage and sue him. Could prove very costly for the record label,' I said.

Verity laughed. 'With all the money he's going to make, I don't think they'll mind. That anti-bullying track alone was incredible.'

My stomach sank. I wasn't exactly crazy about the idea of being a bully. How was I supposed to know he had a complex about his massive schnoz?

After that, we headed to the main stage to wait for the headliner. Ad stood with Jasmeen, Harry with Verity, and me with Mila. I wasn't really in a talkative mood and I think she picked up on it.

'I'm sorry the Natalie thing didn't work,' she said to me. 'Maybe it wasn't meant to be, eh?'

I turned my head so she couldn't see my wobbly lip. 'Yeah, maybe.'

'Hey, I know what would make you feel better.'

I turned and saw her smiling at me. I thought I knew what she was driving at. 'Getting Oh, Inverted World to sign me another photo?'

Her smile disappeared. 'Yeah, probably not.'

'Oh.'

I glanced over at a campfire and someone familiar caught my eye. It had to be Gav. I hadn't seen anyone else at *BUZZFEST* wearing a tracksuit. I couldn't get a good view though because he was in the process of snogging the face off some girl. I KNEW IT! Before I could stop myself, I was walking over there.

I cleared my throat. They didn't stop. They just kept on slurping at each other. It made me feel kind of sick, to be honest.

'Excuse me.'

Still nothing.

'FREE NOODLES HERE!'

Gav stopped immediately and looked up. You should have seen his face—from hope to despair at Warp ten. I wish I'd recorded it. 'What are you doing, man?' he huffed.

'Nothing,' I replied. 'Just thought I'd swing by to say hello.'

'Hi!' The girl beamed at me. 'Do you know my Schmuffy-cakes?'

If I'd have been drinking, it would have shot out of my

« Older posts

nose. 'Schmuffycakes?' I said to Gav.

Gav narrowed his eyes at me and mouthed what were probably silent death threats. 'Yeah, this is Poppy.'

'Poppy!' I said, glad the mystery was finally over. 'It's lovely to meet you. So how long have you and Schmuffycakes been a going concern?'

Gav glared at me as if he wanted to remove my gallbladder with his bare hands.

Poppy grinned and wrinkled her nose. 'Four months, three weeks, two days . . .' She stopped and counted her fingers. 'And seven hours!'

Poppy grabbed Gav's hand and he forced a smile.

'Well now some things are beginning to make sense,' I said. 'My name is Joe—I'm Gav's stepbrother.'

'Aww, Joe!' she screamed. 'I've heard SO MUCH about you!'

'Really?' I said.

'Yeah, all right, all right, he don't need to know about that,' said Gav, kicking empty noodle cartons into the fire.

'Oh, I do,' I said. 'We'll catch up later. Are you coming to the wedding?'

'Wedding?' she said. 'What wedding? You didn't tell me about a wedding, Schmuffycakes.'

I decided to leave them to it. So that's why Gav was being so secretive. He's going out with the most happy-clappy person in the world! She's like the anti-Gav! Ha! This is incredible!

I went back to the others. Something odd was happening.

'Oh cocking hell,' I said. 'Ad, why are you snogging Jasmeen?'

They broke off and Harry, Verity, and Mila booed me as if I were a pantomime villain.

'I've never kissed a gay bloke before,' said Jasmeen. 'I wanted to see what it'd be like, knowing it's doing absolutely nothing for him.'

'Absolutely nothing, eh, Ad?' I said.

Ad's eyes were massive and his mouth hung open. 'Y-yeah, mate. Nothing. I think I need to sit down for a bit.'

He dropped to the floor and Jasmeen joined him.

'What about you, my dear?' said Harry to Verity. 'Care to experiment?'

I eyeballed him. If they're not careful, they're going to get found out.

Verity sighed and spat her chewing gum out. 'Ah, go on then.'

It got a bit awkward then, just me and Mila standing there. I looked at the stage for a distraction, but there was just a tubby bloke going, 'Test, test, test.'

'This is kind of weird, isn't it?' Mila squeezed my hand and nodded at the other two couples carrying out their 'experiments'.

'Yeah,' I said. 'I wish Ad would close his eyes and stop making eye contact with me. It's creeping me out.'

Mila laughed, then gently karate-chopped my arm. 'Hey, I've thought of a distraction.'

'What?' I said. 'Anything.'

'Kiss me.'

Blood rushed to my face yet again. I must have looked like a derelict postbox. Mila looked up at me, her eyes wide and twinkling.

Just do it, you freakin' dork, said Hank.

While I would normally advise against such cavalier reasoning, in this case, I think it would be wise, said Norman. *Who knows, it might help you get over—*

'NATALIE!' I spotted her over Mila's shoulder, walking past with Greeny. Without thinking, I ran over.

'I thought you agreed to leave me alone for the rest of the weekend,' she said, wrapping her arm around Greeny's.

'I just need to explain,' I said. 'I was chased into a Portaloo by Mr Boocock—'

'What, the PE teacher?' said Greeny.

I glared at him and carried on as if he wasn't there. 'The picture I showed you, it was signed by Oh, Inverted World,

HANK

NORMAN

but it got ruined by gallons of crap.'

'Hold on a minute.' Natalie let go of Greeny. 'Where did you get that?'

'eBay, probably,' said Greeny.

'Actually, Quentin,' I said, which is his real first name and I'm not even joking. 'I didn't have to pay a single penny for this item. I met the band myself and got them to sign the picture to Natalie. They even wrote "make it so" on there.'

Natalie gasped, actually gasped. She stepped closer to me, her black-rimmed eyes burning with curiosity, and, possibly, LOVE. 'How did you manage that?'

'Let's just say I have contacts.' I turned around to look at Mila, but she had her back to me and was hugging Verity. Weird.

Natalie stepped closer still and gave me a little smile. 'Well, that's . . .'

'Nat,' said Greeny.

She looked back at him, then shook her head quickly. 'Yeah,' she said. 'You're right.'

'What do you mean he's right?' I said.

Natalie took a deep breath. 'Look, Joe,' she said, 'if that is really what you did, then I appreciate it. It was very thoughtful. But it doesn't change how I feel. I'm sorry.'

She held Greeny's hand and they walked off together. STUPID GREENY! I counted to seven then kicked a discarded pot of noodles. It looped dramatically skywards off

« Older posts

the end of my welly and smacked a hard-looking bloke right in the face and I had to run away quite fast.

When we got back to the campsite, Harry, Ad, Verity, and Jasmeen built a campfire and sat around it. Mila went straight to bed.

'What's the, um, matter with Mila?' I asked.

Jasmeen sucked her teeth. 'You are such a knob, Joe.'

Sorry I asked.

I didn't want to go to bed then, so I sat up with them for a while. I wish I hadn't bothered. At one point, the girls even got me to take some photos of them kissing, because I was the only one with a fully charged phone. I feel I should clarify that last sentence, I mean

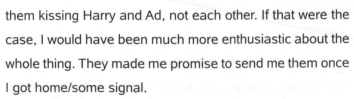

them kissing Harry and Ad, not each other. If that were the case, I would have been much more enthusiastic about the whole thing. They made me promise to send me them once I got home/some signal.

I wasn't really paying attention though. I was too busy thinking about what Natalie said. If a signed picture from Oh, Inverted World wouldn't do it, what would? It would have to be something even better.

Hey, numbnuts, said Hank. *What's that crappy song she loves? Couldn't you get that band of sissies to dedicate it to her or something?*

What a terrific idea. Which is a rare thing from Hank. All I need to do is meet Oh, Inverted World again and get them to dedicate 'Us Against the Universe' to Natalie. Despite their mopey reputations, they seem like an amenable bunch of chaps. Trouble is, there's only one way to get to them.

'Hey, girls,' I said.

'What's up, mate?' said Ad, who had his hand on Jasmeen's leg and wasn't even being subtle about it. 'They're a bit busy at the minute.'

'I just wanted to ask, do you think it would be a good idea for me to go and talk to Mila?'

'It might be, yeah,' said Verity. 'I mean, she did get you backstage to meet that band and stop you from getting your arse kicked by a mental security guard, but other than that, what has she ever done for you?'

I got up and went over to her tent.

'Knock knock,' I said.

'Who's that?' she replied.

'Doctor.'

'What are you talking about, Joe?'

Ah right. They obviously don't have knock knock jokes in Holland.

'Can I come in?' I said. 'I need a word.'

'I'm thinking of a word right now,' said Mila. 'You wouldn't like it.'

I gulped and rubbed my hands on my thighs. 'Look, I'm sorry,' I said. 'I haven't thanked you for all you've done for me and I've been a . . .'

'A klootzak?'

'What does that mean?'

'Never mind.'

The zip opened slowly. 'I will permit you to enter.'

I crawled inside and did the zip back up. Mila hung a torch from the top of the tent. It swung gently and made our shadows wobble on the canvas.

'So . . .' Mila sat cross-legged with her hands in her lap. She was wearing jogging bottoms and a Pink Floyd 'Wish You Were Here' hoodie.

'So . . .' I said back.

'I accept your apology,' she said.

'Great.'

We didn't say anything for a while. The only thing that filled the silence was fragments of the campfire conversation—most worryingly Ad betting them all that he could totally light a fart.

'You know, not many girls are like me,' said Mila.

'What do you mean?'

'Well, I saw you covered head-to-foot in stront and still offered to kiss you.'

I chuckled. 'You're not very picky, are you?'

She laughed and took her hair out of a ponytail, shaking it down onto her shoulders.

'Maybe not,' she said.

We didn't say anything for a while.

'I like you, Joe,' she said.

'Oh,' I said. 'Um, thank you.'

And you wonder why I drink, said Hank.

I didn't know what to say. I mean, this wasn't supposed to happen. I was in that tent for one reason and one reason only—to get access to Oh, Inverted World. Before I could think of a way to change the subject, Mila quickly reached forward, grabbed my shoulder, and kissed me. It was nice. Proper nice. And not just like 'wow, I'm kissing a girl' nice. It was this really warm feeling, like maybe not everyone hates me. Maybe someone can see past the fact that I am a massive stinking cretin.

« Older posts

And I do like Mila—I really do. She's pretty and funny and loves the Floyd and what the cocking hell more do you want in a person?

But she's not Natalie. Like is not love. I couldn't help but think about her. About all the great times we had. That perfect summer day we shared ice creams in the park. The time her lip piercing got stuck in my braces and we had to be cut free by the dentist. When Boocock caught us snogging around the back of the PE supply cupboard and turned a hose on us. She should have been the one I was kissing. I had to remember why I was really there.

Mila rested her forehead against mine and touched my cheek. A chant of 'We know what you're doing,' started around the campfire and soon every idiot in VIP was doing it.

Mila giggled. 'I forget about the shadows.' She held a middle finger up and a big cheer rang out.

'So what do you want to do tomorrow?' she said.

'I don't know,' I said. 'As it's the last day, what's say we head backstage again? That'd be cool, wouldn't it?'

She took her hand off my face, turned the torch off, and lay down.

'Goodnight, Joe,' she said.

Smooth, said Hank.

'But, Mila . . .'

'Just get out of my tent.'

Damn.

I crawled out and hoped to quietly get into mine. The sound of hundreds of people chanting 'You blew it,' at me put paid to that.

2 a.m.

Managed to get some phone reception to look up the translation of klootzak. Can't argue, to be honest.

Sunday 4th August
10 a.m.

Well, this is just MARVELLOUS.

I got out of my tent earlier to find everyone else already up, sitting around a smouldering fire. Mila wouldn't look at me.

'Morning, old boy,' said Harry.

'Yeah, how you doing, mate?' said Ad, offering me a pan of burned beans. 'Want some breakfast?'

I eyeballed them suspiciously. Why were they being so friendly? Something wasn't right.

'What's going on?' I said as I sat down.

'What do you mean, old son?' said Harry. 'Can we not

bid our oldest friend a good morning without him questioning our motives?'

'No,' I said. 'You can't. Now spill it.'

'We know the secret,' Jasmeen blurted out. Verity reached over and gave her leg a playful smack.

I frowned. 'What, that Ad's real name is Adward? I know, I was shocked when I found out, too.'

The others looked at each other with 'oh crap' expressions on their faces.

'No,' said Verity. She leaned forward and whispered, 'We know they're not gay.'

I must have turned purple.

'What the? I mean, how?'

'Come on, do you think we're stupid?' said Jasmeen. 'I caught Ad staring at my cleavage for seventeen seconds.'

'Didn't blink even once,' said Verity.

I facepalmed. 'Fine. But no one can know about this. This has to remain between us.'

Verity saluted. 'We will take it to the grave, soldier.'

God, she's been spending too much time with Harry. I turned on him.

'I expected better of you. You're supposed to be all about strategy.'

Harry shrugged. 'Temptations of the flesh and all that.'

'You have to be discrete though,' I said. 'If you're going

to . . . canoodle. Try to make it seem like you're a camp best friend. Say stuff like "fabulous" and . . . "nice bangers".'

Harry blinked. 'I don't know about anyone else, but I'm still processing the fact that Joe just used the word "canoodle".'

They all laughed. Idiots.

'The last time I went in one of them I fell out and nearly drownded,' said Ad.

'What, old boy?'

'A canoodle.'

I took that as my cue to leave. What do I care, anyway? I'm not even their manager any more. Let them wreck their own careers.

Right, I'm in the tent now, going through my strategy. There has to be a way I can get into the backstage area. This is going to require all of my considerable intellect.

4 p.m.

Who am I kidding? I have no intellect.

I tried to strut up to the entrance as confidently as I could, but then I started overthinking things, and suddenly became very aware that I was walking, and had to consider every step in case I forgot how to do it. Anyway, long story short, I fell over and headbutted the bouncer in the chest.

'I do apologize, my good fellow,' I said.

Hank bit his knuckle.

« Older posts

'I was just wondering if I could enter the backstage area? If you remember, I was here with a young lady only yesterday.'

Yeah, I don't know why I was talking like that either. I guess I was trying to sound all grown up or something.

He frowned. The headbutt didn't seem to affect him. I think it might have concussed me though. 'Yeah, you were with Mila, weren't you?'

'That's right,' I said. 'So, I'll just be on my—'

He stopped me with a King Kong hand. 'No you won't.'

My mouth flapped open and shut like a tapped goldfish. 'But you let me in yesterday.'

'That was because you were with Mila. Get Mila to come here and I'll let you in. Until then, bye-bye.'

I walked away and tried to think. The fences were too tall for me to climb and that man mountain would destroy me if he caught me trying. There had to be another way. Then I saw it—my ticket to victory. A laundry hamper on wheels. I would hide in there and wait for someone to push me inside. I'd seen it in cartoons millions of times.

I took a quick look around and jumped in. Luckily, the cloths and towels in there were clean. It was comfortable, too. I could have fallen asleep. I sat and waited for the next part of my plan to be put into action.

I waited a little longer.

A wasp flew into the hamper and buzzed right up to my face, but I didn't want to give away my position by wafting it away, so I tried to crush it psychologically.

'You're good for nothing, wasp. Do you hear me? NOTHING! At least bees pollinate or whatever it is they do. You just sting, and you do it for fun. You want to watch the world BURN.'

I was just getting to the end of another anti-wasp rant when through a thin split in the side I saw what I thought was my saviour: a bloke in overalls coming from the Porta-loos. He must have left the hamper there while he relieved himself in one of the stinky pits of doom. I hunched down and covered myself in the towels.

After a few seconds, the wheels started to move.

I am surprised this is working, said Norman. *I thought it would be more problematic.*

The wheels stopped.

You just don't know when to shut the hell up, do you, Norm? said Hank.

Everything was dark. My vision was blocked by the towels. Until they were lifted off.

'Gerrout of it, you little bleeder.'

I jumped out of the hamper and ran before the overalls bloke could catch me. Why did I not consider the fact that he might notice the extra weight? TV has lied to me again.

What am I going to do now? If Harry wasn't so obsessed with Verity, he might have been able to help. Hang on, I think I can hear him outside the tent, calling me. What the cocking hell does he want?

2 a.m.

'Where have you bloody been, old boy?' Harry yelled as he dragged me from the tent.

'What's the matter?' I said. 'Ad hasn't had an accident has he?'

Harry stood me up and grabbed me by the shoulders. 'She's had a stroke!' he screamed.

'Well, I'm really happy for you, but what you get up to with Verity is no business of mine,' I said.

'Not Verity, you bloody fool,' he said. 'Flossie!'

I searched my memory banks but came away empty-handed.

'Flossie the DJ granny who won the competition!' said Harry.

'Oh,' I said. 'OH. So that means . . .'

Harry grabbed my face and planted a massive sloppy kiss on my forehead. 'We're playing *BUZZFEST*, old boy! TONIGHT!'

'Jesus,' I said. 'But what about all your gear?'

Harry bounced up and down. I had never seen him like this before. 'They're flying it in by helicopter, soldier. Helicopter! Do you have any idea how exciting this is?'

'It's amazing,' I said. 'But, you know, poor Flossie and that.'

'Yeah, it's a shame, but they say she'll be OK,' said Harry. 'Anyway, old bean, that's not all. Because we are now performers, we have certain privileges . . .'

« Older posts

He pulled a laminated piece of paper on a lanyard out of his pocket and my stomach nearly pogoed out of my oesophagus.

Oh my cocking God. You should have seen that guard when I waved that bad boy in his face. He was FUMING!

When I got into the backstage area, I tried to remember where Oh, Inverted World's trailer was. I hoped they'd still be there, as they were due on stage pretty soon. I knew that even with all the *SOUND EXPERIENCE* excitement, there was no way Natalie would miss them.

I weaved in and out of the trailers until I finally found their caravan. I knocked on the door and waited. Eventually, it opened.

'Yeah?' The guy wearing eyeliner squinted at me.

'Hi there,' I said. 'Sorry to bother you again. It's Joe—Mila's friend.'

I felt a stab of guilt but tried to submerge it. I had to focus on my Grand Gesture.

He screwed his face up. 'Oh yeah, what's up?'

'I was just wondering . . .' I looked around, 'if you could do me a favour.'

He shrugged. 'We've got to play a show soon, so . . .'

'That's kind of what I wanted to talk to you about,' I said. 'Can I come in?'

The bloke studied me as if I were some kind of alien, then jerked his head back. 'All right, John, come on in.'

I walked in and saw two of the band playing *Epic Warfare* against each other. The other one was pacing around and doing vocal warm-ups. Either that or attempting to summon a demon.

'So, what can we do for you, man?' said the guy who let me in.

'I was just wondering if you could dedicate a song to someone for me.'

Epic Warfare paused and they turned around. The other bloke stopped trying to raise Beelzebub/mucus.

'Look, dude,' he said. 'We ain't Barry Manilow.'

'No one was accusing you of being him,' I said, making a mental note to find out who the cocking hell Barry Manilow is. 'It's just really important.'

The bloke who let me in took a long drag on a stubby cigarette. 'Why?' he said.

'It's kind of a long story.'

'Well, tell it,' said the devil guy. He sat down and lit up a cigarette of his own.

'Yeah, and make it entertaining 'cause I just swallowed some pills and they're making me drowsy,' said one of the blokes on the couch.

'Awesome, what were they?' the other one asked.

'Hayfever meds,' he replied.

These bands aren't quite as rock and roll as they make themselves out to be. Anyway, I took a deep breath and told them my story. Told them everything. About Natalie and Lisa, and jumping off the roof into Boocock, and slapping Data dressed as Picard, and singing about being gay on regional news, and getting covered in the poo of a thousand people. Everything. By the time I was done, they were all in tears. Of laughter.

'All right, all right,' said one of them. 'We'll dedicate a song to your girl.'

'Yeah, that was the best God damn story I've ever heard,' said another.

I smiled. I couldn't believe I'd done it. 'Can you make it "Us Against the Universe"?' I said.

'Sure, sure, whatever you want, man,' said the blue-haired guy, chuckling. 'Covered in festival crap. That is classic.'

I practically skipped out of the caravan. This one had to work. I could tell Natalie was impressed by me getting the signed photo—it was only that knobber Greeny being there that stopped her forgiving me. When this masterpiece went off, there would be nothing he could do.

I turned a corner and crashed into someone coming the other way. I mumbled sorry and carried on, too buzzing about my Grand Gesture to stop.

'Hey.'

I turned around. My buzz flew off a cliff.

'Oh,' I said. 'Hello.'

Troy stood there with this kind of embarrassed smile on his face.

'I guess you know my big secret now,' he said.

'What, that you used our confidential sessions to write a stupid rap?' I said. 'I ought to have you struck off the bloody counselling register thing. Still, I bet they haven't got round to putting you on it yet, since you only qualified five minutes ago.'

He put his hands on his hips, that smile still on his face. 'I quit,' he said.

'What?'

He shrugged. 'It wasn't for me. I let you get under my skin far too easily. I realized that the only way for me to deal with my issues was to channel them into my music. I suppose I should thank you, really. Meeting you gave me the kick up the backside I needed.'

'I'd like to give you a real kick up the backside,' I mumbled.

'Sorry?'

'Nothing.'

'Anyway, it might well pay off soon,' he said. 'I heard some record companies might be interested in signing me.'

'Yeah, I heard that, too,' I said. 'See you around then.'

'Wait,' he called me back. I stopped. 'One last word of

« Older posts

advice: if you want to get better, try to channel your issues into something creative like I did.'

I laughed. 'You mean something like writing a blog?'

He gave me a thumbs up. 'Yeah, awesome. That'll help!'

I shot back with a thumbs up of my own. 'Course it will.'

Troy held out his hand. 'All the best, Joe.'

I reluctantly shook it. I hate the idea of being name-checked in a rap, but I suppose I wasn't exactly the best patient in the world.

'I hope things get better soon,' he said.

'After today they will,' I said. 'I guarantee it.'

'Wow,' said Troy with a little chuckle. 'What's happening today then?'

'A Grand Gesture,' I replied. 'The Grandest Gesture of all time.'

He looked at me like I was mental, but I didn't care.

I turned the corner by the trailer and saw Harry, Ad, Greeny, Verity, Jasmeen, Natalie, and Mila standing together. I ran over.

'Hi, everybody!' I yelled.

Both Natalie and Mila ignored me. Excellent. Hated by two girls. This could be a new personal best.

Don't sweat it, man, said Hank. *This is all gonna change.*

I knew he was right.

'Greetings, old boy,' said Harry. 'Just cobbling together a set list for the big show.'

'Actually, mate,' said Ad, 'there was something we wanted to ask you.'

I looked at him, suddenly aware that I'd been staring at Natalie. 'What?'

'Do you want to come up and do "Gay as the Day Is Long" as an encore?'

My mouth dried up like I'd swallowed a sandpit. My legs felt like they were made of spaghetti.

'No way,' I said. 'I'm never doing that again.'

'Come on, old boy,' said Harry. 'This is a huge opportunity!'

'No,' I said, firmer this time. 'I'm going to leave the performing to you two.'

'Um, I think you'll find there are three of them,' said Natalie.

I chuckled. 'Well, if you count messing about with a projector as being a member of the band, then yes, I suppose there are three.'

Everyone looked pissed off with me. Whatever. I didn't care. All I could think about was the Grand Gesture.

'Anyway,' said Natalie. 'I'm going to go and get a good spot for Oh, Inverted World. I'll see you guys later.'

'I'll come with you!' I said.

She brushed her fringe out of her eyes. 'Actually, I think I'd rather go alone,' she said, and quickly walked away.

Mila raised her eyebrows at me. I didn't know what to

say, so I just smiled, then followed Natalie.

I made sure to keep her in sight, but not get close enough for her to know I was there. I felt like a detective on a stakeout.

Or a stalker on a stalkout.

Shut up, Hank.

When she got to her spot, I stood a few paces behind. The idea was, when the band dedicated the song to her from me, I would swoop in and she would look into my eyes and realize that I was her one true love, and

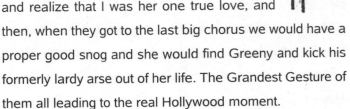

HANK

then, when they got to the last big chorus we would have a proper good snog and she would find Greeny and kick his formerly lardy arse out of her life. The Grandest Gesture of them all leading to the real Hollywood moment.

This thrash metal band called Flameboy were on stage. They didn't really do it for me, but the rest of the crowd seemed to be enjoying it. So much so that they were forming a big circle and beating the hell out of each other. It just seems like a waste of money to me. If I want to fight strangers whilst listening to what sounds like a tramp throwing up, I'll just go down the park on a Saturday night.

Anyway, after they left the stage, these blokes in black T-shirts came on and started setting up Oh, Inverted World's gear. When their big crying angel backdrop went up, so did my heart rate. This was going to be amazing.

Loads more people started squeezing into the arena. Emos as far as the eye could see. What is the collective term for group of emos, anyway? A sigh? I don't know.

The swelling crowd began to push me further away from Natalie, so I repositioned myself more to the left of her. It was riskier, but I knew once the band were on stage, she wouldn't be able to take her eyes off them.

I was so glad Greeny wasn't there. And he wasn't there because the 𝘚𝘖𝘜𝘕𝘋 𝘌𝘟𝘗𝘌𝘙𝘐𝘌𝘕𝘊𝘌 were preparing for their gig. And they only had a gig in the first place because Flossie had dropped out. So basically, what I'm saying is, I was glad an old lady had a stroke. I am a terrible human being.

I was still looking at Natalie when a massive roar came up from the crowd. It rattled my eardrums and vibrated my brain. The band were walking on stage. A smile spread across Natalie's face.

Straight away, they launched into a song I'm pretty sure was called 'Avalanche of Feelings'. The crowd surged forward and pushed me so hard I nearly fell. This big emo stopped me mid-tumble and gave me a solemn nod. Through all the swaying and pushing, I made sure I could see Natalie at all times. Despite being jostled all over the place, she had this really peaceful look on her face. She looked beautiful.

« Older posts

I recognized the next song they played, too. In fact, I recognized all of them. Natalie was always blasting their albums. Every song brought back a different memory. The first time she told me she really liked me. That time we rode our bikes to the reservoir. When we sat on the bus on the way back from Water World, sharing her earphones. I can still remember the feeling of her damp hair on my neck.

I realized I'd been standing there grinning like an idiot. I must have been doing it for their whole set. Natalie caught my eye and, for a split second, she smiled at me. I could tell she was thinking about the same stuff. We were reliving it together. It was magical—telepathy powered by music. Then her expression clouded over and she looked back at the stage. Damn.

The point was, though, the music was working even though she didn't want it to. I really needed the Grand Gesture to pay off. Every time they finished a song, my stomach would turn over. They had to play it. They promised. I started to edge closer to Natalie.

'Right, guys, the next song we're gonna play is like, very special,' the lead singer said.

'Earlier today, we met this guy called John.'

I facepalmed.

'And he told us this cool story about how he had an amazing girl, but screwed up and lost her. We can all relate to that, right?'

Loads of miserable-looking emos cheered.

'Anyway, it was the best friggin' story we'd ever heard, so we said we'd dedicate this song to his special girl.'

I saw Natalie looking at me. I'm sure there was a hint of a smile on her lips. I started moving closer, squeezing through gaps in the throng.

'So this is for you, Lisa.'

I think my heart actually stopped for a second. The crowd cheered.

« Older posts

'You're way better than that bitch Natalie.'

Natalie's mouth dropped open and before I could get to her she was away, pushing through the crowd. I called her name but 'Us Against the Universe' drowned me out.

He got the God damn names wrong! Hank screamed. *That make-up wearing sissy son of a—*

Um, maybe next time, you should submit the request in writing, said Norman.

Next time? There isn't going to be a next time. It's over.

I left the arena. The sun was setting, making everything look all orange. Even that bloke in a thong who had by this point scrawled 'End War' on his bum cheeks looked kind of majestic. Not that I was in the mood for any of that. I just kept walking. I wanted to get away from everything. *BUZZFEST* was supposed to be the best thing ever, but it turned out to be the worst.

I trudged past the VIP campsite and up onto the hill. This seemed like a good idea at the time, but once I got up there, I realized it was nothing but couples canoodling. I don't care what Harry says, there is nothing wrong with that word.

I was stepping over some sprawled bodies when I heard someone calling me. I turned around and saw Poppy grinning and waving, and Gav looking like he wanted to die.

They were having a picnic. I went over.

'You know, I was just saying to Gavin, that boy looks like Joe,' she said. 'And he was insisting it wasn't, but I knew it was, didn't I, Schmuffycakes?'

Gav shrugged.

'Uh oh, looks like Mr Grumpy is back!' She started tickling him and I could tell he was trying not to laugh.

'Would you like to join us, Joe?' she asked. 'We've got LOADS of couscous left. Gavin loves couscous, don't you?'

'No,' he mumbled. 'Don't even know what it is.'

'Liar liar. Pants. On. Fire,' said Poppy, prodding Gav on the end of his nose after every word.

'What do you want anyway, man?' said Gav.

'Just come for a walk,' I said. 'Needed some time to think.'

'Ah, you can't beat a good think, can you?' said Poppy. 'You know, you and my Schmuffycakes are so alike. He is a very deep thinker.'

I glanced at Gav. He gave me a look as if to say, 'Correct her and I'll kick you into the sun.'

Poppy leaned over and jabbed my kneecap. 'Are you sure I can't interest you in some couscous?'

'Uh, no thanks,' I said. 'Anyway, are you guys going to watch the *SOUND EXPERIENCE*?'

'What do you mean?' said Gav. 'Watch them do what?'

'Play the dance stage,' I said. 'Haven't you heard?'

'No way, man, that's mental,' said Gav.

'Schmuffycakes told me all about the $SOUND$ $EXPERI$-$ENCE$ and how he was their bodyguard,' said Poppy. 'I can't believe anyone could be scared of him. He's such a big teddy bear.'

I smiled, which felt weird. 'Really?' I said. 'Tell me more about Schmuffycakes's teddy-bear qualities.'

'Anyway,' said Gav, a bit too quick. 'Let's go then, yeah? We want to get a good spot, don't we?'

He stood up, and pulled Poppy up with him.

'Aren't you an eager beaver?' she said. 'But you're right. I can't wait to see them. Ooh, look at you, Gavin, hobnobbing with famous people. I could get used to this glamorous showbiz life.'

We got to the dance tent early. I think Gav just wanted to be somewhere loud where Poppy couldn't tell me that he likes to skip through flowery meadows in a dress or something like that.

I looked at my backstage pass and thought about seeing how they were getting on. I decided against it in the end. The last thing they'd need was me flapping around them when they were trying to get ready for the biggest gig of their lives. Besides, they said it themselves, I'm not their manager any more.

I looked at my watch. Half an hour until they were due on. It seemed like news of the $SOUND$ $EXPERIENCE$ replacing Flossie had filtered through, because I kept hearing snippets of conversations about them. God, they're more famous than I thought.

I started thinking back to how I got myself into this whole mess. That night at the Silk Kitty in London. If I'd have just stayed calm, it wouldn't have happened. I wouldn't have met Lisa by the fountain and we wouldn't . . . well, you know the rest.

I thought about that slimy git, Seb. Does he have any idea how much he wrecked my life when he put up those pictures of him and Natalie during his DJ set? Even if he did, he wouldn't care. He's going to Cambridge University in September. I hear he has ambitions to become Prime Minister. If that happens, I'm leaving the country. No, the planet.

Thinking about Seb stirred something in my brain though. If he could wreak such misery with a couple of measly photos, who was to say I couldn't put things right with some photos of my own?

I paced around at the back, trying to weigh up how it could possibly go wrong. It couldn't. It was completely foolproof.

I pushed through the crowd until I got to the sound desk in the middle of the tent. I flashed my pass at the bouncer and he let me in. There were a couple of blokes in there eating noodles. They both had ponytails, and yet were completely bald on top.

'What do you want?' said Ponytail One.

'I'm the SOUND EXPERIENCE's manager,' I said, which was only a little white lie.

'You are?' said Ponytail Two. 'You look a little young to be a manager.'

'And you look a little old to be wearing leather trousers,' I replied.

Ponytail Two sat down and started chomping on his noodles.

'I need to make a late addition to the SOUND EXPERIENCE'S AV,' I said, trying my best to sound like a pro.

'Oh yeah?' Ponytail One raised an eyebrow.

'Yes,' I said. 'I need you to put some pictures up on the big screen for me.'

He huffed. 'When?'

'When I go up on stage and give you the order.' I pulled my phone out and scrolled to the pictures I wanted. 'Use these.'

I passed him my phone. He nearly dropped it because of the noodle juice on his fingers. Idiot. When he had a proper grip on it, he put on a pair of glasses and squinted at the screen. 'You mean these ones with all the kissing?' he said.

'That's right,' I said. 'Any questions?'

'Have the band agreed to this?' he said.

'Hey.' I blasted him with a finger pistol. 'The band agrees

to whatever I tell them to agree to.'

He connected my phone to his laptop and downloaded the images before giving it back. I then left the sound desk and went back to Gav and Poppy. I thought I was going to throw up. The roadies were on stage, setting up the *SOUND EXPERIENCE*'s gear. I stared straight ahead, going through what I was about to do.

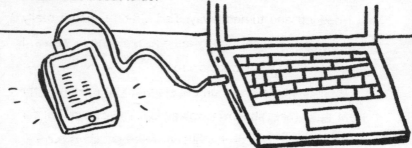

As time went on, more and more people crammed into the tent. There must have been about five thousand in there. I closed my eyes and rubbed my temples. I tried to repeat that chant Natalie taught me to help me beat stage fright.

Be like Picard.

Be like Picard.

Be like Picard.

When I opened my eyes, Natalie was in front of me. Or at least the back of her head was. She was talking to Gav and Poppy. I tapped her on the shoulder. She turned around slowly.

'What do you want now?'

« Older posts

'I'm sorry about the band getting your name wrong,' I said.

'Just don't talk to me,' she said.

'But, Natalie—'

'Joe, I am here to watch the guys play *BUZZFEST*. This is a big moment and I'm not going to let you ruin it, OK?'

I nodded and turned away. This Grand Gesture really was my last chance. I had messed up too many times. I couldn't allow anything to go wrong.

The lights went down on the stage and a massive roar went up. Three shadows walked out. I was terrified for them. Ad must have filled eight buckets with all his puke.

They started 'Kamikaze Attackk' and sounded amazing. At least I think they did—I still don't really get their music. The whole experience would have been better without Greeny's so-called 'visuals' but whatever.

I pushed through the mad, dancing crowd and got out of the tent. I sprinted around to the gate, flashed my pass at the bouncer, and got backstage. Verity, Jasmeen, and Mila were watching from the side.

'They are AMAZING, aren't they?' said Jasmeen.

I looked at the stage and saw Harry furiously twiddling dials and chewing his pipe, Ad squinting at his 808 as he bashed it, and that idiot Greeny pressing buttons on his effects console.

'Yeah, they are,' I said.

'Are you sure you don't want to do "Gay as the Day Is Long"?' said Verity. 'It will be epic. If I were you, I'd totally do it.'

'If you were comfortable with your sexuality, you'd do it,' said Jasmeen. 'Isn't that right, Mila?'

She shrugged and wouldn't make eye contact.

'I'm comfortable with my sexuality, I'm just not comfortable with looking like a knob in front of thousands of people.'

'Says the guy who ran through the site covered in poo,' said Jasmeen.

I ignored them and stared at the stage. The crowd bounced. My intestines tied themselves into the kind of complicated knot you'd earn a Scout badge for.

After every track, I'd go to make my entrance, but I couldn't move.

Look, Joe, said Norman. *I've been rather quiet up until now, but enough is enough. How many of these Grand Gestures are you going to attempt before you admit defeat?*

DEFEAT? Hank yelled, throwing a chair at the wall. *We don't know the meaning of the word!*

Norman leaned forward, his hands on the control panel. *This will end badly. You know it, I know it, even this swivel-eyed buffoon next to me knows it.*

HEY! Hank cried. *Who are you calling a baboon?*

See what I mean?

« Older posts

I wavered on the edge of the stage. The song was coming to an end. I had to make a decision.

Look, man, do you love this chick or not? said Hank.

'Of course I do,' I said out loud.

Then you can't wuss out now, he said. *This is your last chance!*

I closed my eyes and took a deep breath.

Be like Picard.

Be like Picard.

Be like Picard.

I walked out on stage. Ad saw me and his face lit up. Harry winked and passed me a mic.

'Good evening, ladies and gentlemen,' I said.

There was a cheer, followed by a 'Gay as the Day Is Long' chant. I gestured for them to stop, and they did. Eventually.

My eye twitched and my left knee shook. The more I tried to stop it, the worse it got.

'I will perform that song for you,' I said.

WHAT? yelled Hank.

'But first, I just want to show you all something.'

A murmur rippled through the crowd.

'Ponytail One, please do the honours,' I said.

Did you really just call him Ponytail One? Norman groaned, watching through his fingers.

I closed my eyes. The chatter in the crowd got louder.

'Natalie Tuft—'

The chatter turned to booing. What the hell was their problem? Natalie didn't deserve to be booed! I opened my eyes just in time to duck a polystyrene cup filled with some kind of yellow liquid. Then a bottle pinged off my temple. Another smacked me in the chest. I turned around. Harry, Ad, and Greeny stood there staring at me with expressions of unearthly horror on their faces. Behind them, the big screen showed the pictures from my phone.

The wrong pictures from my phone.

They had put up photos of a couple kissing, but it wasn't me and Natalie.

It was Harry and Verity. Then Ad and Jasmeen.

I told you it would end badly, said Norman.

The booing was the loudest thing I had ever heard. Until

the chanting started:

'LIARS, LIARS, LIARS!'

Harry jumped off the riser and grabbed me by the shoulders. 'Why would you do this? What is wrong with you?'

'But . . . but it was an accident!'

'YOU IDIOT! YOU'VE RUINED EVERYTHING!'

A hailstorm of bottles pelted us from every angle. I put up my hands to shield my face and felt the mic being prised away.

'STOP! STOP!' Greeny screamed.

They wouldn't. They were furious. It looked like a riot was about to break out. Two blokes tried to storm the stage and had to be held back by security. Greeny ran back up to the decks and pressed some buttons, creating an ear-shattering drone that is still buzzing around my head now. The noise stopped.

'It's true,' he said into the mic. 'Harry and Ad are not gay.'

The booing started again.

'WAIT!' he yelled. The noise dropped off slightly.

'Harry and Ad are not gay.' He stopped and gulped. 'But I am.'

Oh.

It was as if all the blood had left my head. I felt like I had to sit down.

Greeny walked down from the decks and stood at the lip of the stage. It was so quiet, you could hear his footsteps.

'I've been gay all my life,' he said. 'And I couldn't accept it—just wanted to be like everyone else so I tried to fight it, tried to convince myself that I'd snap out of it, but I couldn't. I even used to accuse other kids of being gay, as if it would stop people finding out the truth about me.'

He walked over to me and put his hand on my shoulder. 'He doesn't know this, but for years, I really liked this boy.'

Oh my God. Surely not? I tried to process all this new information while memories of the Easter prom last year came zooming back like spinning newspaper headlines.

'I liked you,' he said to me. 'Proper liked you.'

'I knew he would never feel the same about me, regardless of how much I teased him,' Greeny went on.

I glanced at him and he gave me a thin smile.

'It was only recently I've been able to come to terms with who I am,' he said. 'And I couldn't have done it without the best friend I've ever had—Natalie.'

A round of applause started. Gradually, it spread until it became a cheer.

'She had her heart broken by Joe,' he went on. 'And one night, we were alone, sitting on this bench outside our school. She was crying and said she felt like she'd never stop. I didn't know what to say to make her feel better. And it just, it just came out of my mouth. Since then, we've helped each other through everything.'

I couldn't believe what I was hearing. I had been driving

« Older posts

myself mad at the thought of them being together and all along I was the reason for it.

Someone in the crowd yelled, 'We love you, Greeny!'

Greeny smiled and held up his hand.

'I learned a lot from Natalie. She taught me not to give a crap about what other people think,' he said. 'She taught me to take care of myself, and she taught me to be proud of who I am.'

A 'Natalie' chant started.

'And mainly, she taught me that it is great to be as gay as the day is long.'

A huge cheer erupted. I got off stage fast. Harry and Ad ran back to the decks. 'Gay as the Day Is Long' boomed around the tent, with Greeny on vocals and thousands of people chanting it back at him.

I got out of the backstage area and away from the tent as quickly as I could. I couldn't face going back to see Natalie. I had given Greeny such a hard time about stealing her from me, when really he was just being nice to her. The two of them were there for each other during a tough time and I was just making it tougher. I am a knob of the highest rank.

That speech he made, too. It was from the heart. Authentic. That was a real Grand Gesture.

I went straight back to my tent and started packing my stuff. It didn't go in the bag the way it came out and half of it was bulging out of the end, but I didn't care. I called Mum

« Older posts

and asked if she could pick me up. She said she'd send Jim.

I was psyching myself up for carrying everything to the car park when I heard a voice behind me:

'Thought I might find you here.'

I turned around and there was Mila. Her wavy blonde hair was blowing in the breeze.

'Hi.'

She smiled. 'You're a real idiot, Joe.'

I laughed under my breath. 'I know.'

'But I definitely won't forget you in a hurry.'

I didn't say anything. I don't think anyone in that tent will forget about what a moron I am.

'Well . . .' Mila held out her hand. 'It's been interesting.'

I shook her hand. 'That's one word for it.'

'Take care of yourself,' she said.

'Thanks. You too.'

I went to walk away, but she spoke again. I turned around.

'Try not to get too hung up on Natalie,' she said. 'I don't want you to go crazy. Crazier.'

I nodded. 'Good advice.'

We said our goodbyes and I hobbled away, lugging all my

crap. I had left the stuffed zombie on the blackened wood that used to be the campfire. I thought it would look dead poetic and symbolic, but then a drunk bloke took a massive run up and punted it into a puddle of sick.

I'm writing this in the back of Jim's car. Gav texted me and told me that he was getting a lift back with a 'friend'. He then followed that up with another message saying if I told anyone the identity of that 'friend', he would 'fill me in'. I don't know what that means, but it's probably not pleasant.

'Us Against the Universe' has just come on the radio. I've asked Jim to switch it off. I never want to hear it again.

Friday 9th August

Highlights of the week

- Having to change the twins' nappies.
- Dry-heaving into the bin after the above occurred.
- Looking at pictures of Natalie and feeling sorry for myself.
- Staying inside for so long that I've forgotten what non-stinky air is like.

So as you can tell, it's been a pretty crappy few days.

I have been avoiding calls from everyone. I just don't want to face the world. I mean, is there anyone's life I

« Older posts

haven't ruined? I made Greeny confess his big secret in front of everyone and I wrecked Harry and Ad's career before it had even got going. I made Natalie's entire weekend a misery, and that's without even mentioning Mila. She was the only person who could make me forget Natalie and I treated her like crap.

Luckily, with the wedding looming, I've been able to shut myself away without Mum bothering me. There is so much stuff to organize that she doesn't have time—flowers, food, transport. All kinds of things I'd never even thought about. Apparently, the SOUND EXPERIENCE are still doing the reception, even though they're probably a national disgrace. I hope they blame it all on me because I deserve it.

I was lying on my bed staring at the crack in my ceiling, which now stretches from end to end, when there was a knock at the front door. I ignored it. Someone else would get it.

Another knock—louder this time.

I groaned and stumbled downstairs. It looked like everyone was out. Great, I have to do EVERYTHING.

On the way down, I thought it might have been all right if it was those Mormon lads I've seen going around the estate on their bikes. They've been forced to leave wherever it is they live in America to try to convert the people of Tammerstone, including Mad Morris, who responded to their attempts by emptying a bin over their heads and calling them 'Satan's messengers'. I suppose what I'm trying to say is, I wanted to talk to someone worse off than me.

I opened the door. I was disappointed. It was definitely not Mormons.

'Hello, Dad,' I said. 'What's up?'

Dad stood there frowning. He was alone, without Svetlana or Hercules.

'Can I come in?' he asked.

I nodded and led him through to the lounge. There was something not right about this. For one thing, he never calls at the house, I always go to him. For another, he had just uttered a normal sentence like any normal dad. He didn't call me Pimp Mastah, or offer to take me 'cruising down da Westsiiiiide'.

'Mum and Jim are out,' I said.

Dad sat down and nodded. 'I know,' he said.

'What do you mean you know?'

Dad ignored my question and picked up a framed photo that was sitting on a table. It was of me, Mum, Jim, Gav, and the twins. He smiled sadly and put it back.

« Older posts

'So, it's the big day tomorrow, eh?'

I sat down in the chair near the window.

'Um, yes.'

Dad leaned forward and clasped his hands together. 'And how do you feel about that?'

I shrugged. 'I don't know how I feel about anything. I live in a constant state of misery.'

Dad nodded as if he understood. 'And would that change if . . .' He stared at me, as if he was searching for the right words.

I rubbed my temples. 'You trailed off,' I said. 'I don't have the energy for trailing off and I certainly don't have the energy to finish your sentences for you.'

Dad sat back. He crossed his legs one way and then the other. Then he stood up.

'I'll never forget how I proposed to your mother,' he said.

'Oh-kay,' I said, picking up my phone so I could subtly google whether these were the symptoms of some kind of head injury.

'We were in New York,' he said. 'Central Park—riding in a horse-drawn carriage. It was a crisp winter's evening. The sun was setting and the lamps were beginning to light. You could see them twinkling in the distance, like tiny stars. I knew it was the right time. Perfect. I pulled out the ring. You should have seen her face, son. She was . . .' He stopped and shook his head. 'Have you ever had the feeling that you've made a huge mistake?'

'All the time,' I said. 'But I don't really know what—'

'Never mind,' said Dad. 'Thanks for this.'

He headed for the door.

'Thanks for what?' I yelled after him. 'Do I need to call a brain doctor?'

He didn't reply, just jogged to his convertible and drove away.

Every day, that man finds new ways to be weirder.

Saturday 10th August

Woke up this morning to the sight of the Grim Reaper looming over me. It had finally happened: my heart had actually broken and I had carked it.

'I will come with you, Dark Lord,' I murmured. 'I am ready for what awaits.'

'What the bloody hell you going on about, you soft git?' said Death.

Then my eyes adjusted and I realized it was Chips. To be honest, I didn't know which one was worse.

'Ugh, are you smoking in my

« <u>Older posts</u>

bedroom?' I groaned.

'Never mind that, slaphead,' he puffed. 'Time to go. We've got a wedding to prepare for. You too, Gav.'

'Gizza drag of that,' Gav mumbled.

'Wait a minute, how old are you?' said Chips.

'Sixteen,' said Gav.

'All right, I'll allow it,' he replied, and passed Gav the fag. Unbelievable.

Anyway, we were bundled into a car and whisked away to Chips's house. Jim was already there after kipping in the spare room.

'It's tradition,' Chips explained. 'Can't let the bride and groom knock boots the night before their wedding.'

'One,' I said, 'I would appreciate it if you didn't talk about my mother "knocking boots" and two . . . well, there isn't a two, just never refer to my mum's sex life ever again.'

Chips chuckled to himself and blew a plume of smoke out of the window. 'You know, I heard they booked a honeymoon suite at the hotel tonight. Got a hot tub and everything. I'm sure they'll wear bathers at all times though.'

I stuck my fingers in my ears and fought the urge to vom.

I can already tell that today is going to be fun, fun, FUN!

11 a.m.

Everyone is here now. Jim and Chips are throwing back shots of whisky to 'calm their nerves', and Granddad

Arnold and the Colonel are trading stories about the olden days. It seems like they're trying to one-up each other at times.

> COLONEL: I was shot in the leg and nearly starved to death in a Japanese prisoner-of-war camp.
>
> GRANDAD: Oh yeah? Well I died on the Titanic! Or something like that.

Meanwhile, I can hear Gav on the phone to Poppy, desperately but subtly trying to convince her not to come to the wedding.

'It's going to be well rubbish,' he's saying. 'The do is in a room at our old school. And they're serving peanut stuff . . . Oh, I thought you were allergic to them. What's gluten? Ah, I bet there's going to be loads of that. No, of course I want you to come, bumblebee.'

I'm making a mental note to use 'bumblebee' against him at a later date.

Anyway, I'd better stop writing because the Colonel and Granddad keep tutting at me and saying stuff about young people these days being too reliant on technology and how things were better in the good old days. EVEN THOUGH ALL THEY'VE BEEN CACKING ON ABOUT IS HOW BAD IT WAS IN THE GOOD OLD DAYS.

« Older posts

3 p.m.

I'm back in my room now. There is a bit of time between the wedding ceremony and the reception and I just need to be on my own for a while. I mean, you can't expect me to spend an entire day AND night with my extended family. I swear to Picard, if Great-Uncle Cyril steals my nose one more time, I'm going to steal his Zimmer frame.

Anyway, speaking of old ruins, the Abbey looked really great today. I was sceptical at first because of the simple fact that it doesn't have a roof, but now I can see why Mum and Jim picked it as a wedding venue. It was nicely decorated with flowers and lights and the weather was warm with clear blue skies. There was a kind of altar set up at the head of what would have been the main room with rows of chairs facing it. It was mine and Gav's jobs as ushers to tell people which side to sit. It was basically like working at the cinema, except I didn't get to carry a torch and kick people out who had their pants down in the back row.

Guests soon started to arrive, some of whom I didn't recognize, some of whom I did, and some of whom I did but wished I didn't (people like Uncle Johnny who as his plus one had brought a dummy called Esmeralda). Me and Gav were all 'Bride or groom? Bride or groom?' We got to a point after about ten minutes when we realized that we hadn't agreed on which side was which, but it was too late to change it.

You should have seen Gav's face when Poppy turned up. She was wearing a flowery dress and pink horn-rimmed glasses. I thought she looked weirdly cool.

'Hey, Schmuffycakes!' she screamed, covering Gav's face with red lipstick marks. Gav glanced around to make sure no one was looking. I'm going to let you in on a secret, blog. EVERYONE was looking.

'Yeah, y'alright?' Gav murmured.

'Oh, don't you look handsome in your suit?' she yelled. 'If it is possible, I now fancy you even MORE!'

Gav scratched his face as if he were being attacked by flesh-eating fleas. 'Yeah, cool,' he said. 'Anyway, let's get you sat down, shall we?'

Poppy put on this exaggerated pout and saluted Gav. 'Yes, Mr Usher sir. I will do whatever you say—please don't punish me!'

I hope this lasts because she is amazing. I was laughing so hard as he led her away that I didn't notice the two fig-ures walking up the path to the Abbey. I wasn't sure it was them to begin with—they were wearing suits I had never seen them in before—but as they got closer, little details confirmed it. Glasses. A pipe.

My fight or flight instinct kicked in and flight won by a mile. I had wrecked their lives with my stupid Grand Gesture attempt. Even though I totally deserved it, I knew I couldn't cope with the onslaught from Harry. I quickly walked away, pushing my stupid top hat down so it nearly covered my eyes. I hurried through the east wing of the Abbey until I found a wall about two metres high. I crept behind it and waited, listening for Harry demanding to know where I was hiding. I didn't hear anything, but with Harry being a military strategist, he could have been sneaking up on me like a ninja. I left it a couple of minutes before heading back. When I got there, Gav was fuming.

'Hey, if I don't desert, you don't, you freak,' he said.

'Sorry,' I said. 'I just didn't want to see Harry and Ad.'

'Why not?' he said, still trying to rub the lipstick off his face. 'Is it 'cause you told the whole world that they weren't gay?'

'Yeah, something like that.'

Gav stepped closer to me. The flow of guests had pretty much stopped and the Abbey was nearly full. 'Well, I don't know much, but one thing I do know is if you made a mistake, you've got to try to put it right. You taught me that.'

I laughed to myself. 'I've made so many, I don't know if I'll ever have time. And when I try to put them right, I just end up making things worse.'

Gav looked around and put his hand on my shoulder, violating his own 'no touching unless it's punching' rule. 'If you ask me, you've been trying too hard: getting on stage, dressing up as **STAR TREK** characters. Just keep it simple. Talk to them and hear what they have to say.'

I gulped. I couldn't believe this was what I had come to: taking life advice from Gav.

'Cheers, Gav,' I said.

'S'alright, he said. 'I meant what I said though. I've learned a lot from you, and it ain't just **STAR TREK** stuff neither.'

I didn't know how to respond to that. Gav has literally never said a nice thing about me ever.

'I suppose what I'm trying to say is, I don't mind that we're going to be brothers.'

I looked up at his big, monobrowed face. It's hard to believe that it's the same person who used to call me names and dangle me over dirty toilet bowls for fun.

'I don't mind either,' I said.

'Hey up, ushers.' Chips ducked out of the Abbey. 'We're ready to go so get your arses in here.'

We headed to our seats just behind the front row. Jim turned around and gave us both a nervous nod and smile. Grandma Arnold held onto Holly and Ivy's pushchair. They were wearing little white dresses which looked nice, except for the fact that I think Holly had been sick down hers. Yeah, she definitely takes after me. Luckily, both of them looked like they were staying quiet.

The string quartet in the corner started playing and

everyone stood up. I turned around. There was Mum, walking in with Granddad Arnold. She was wearing this white lace dress with sparkly diamonds on it. Now, I know this sounds weird because she's my mum and everything, but she looked beautiful. Happy, too. It made me feel dead proud, which was weird because I don't often feel that when it comes to my family.

'Mum looks . . .' I murmured out loud.

'Fit,' said Gav.

I shot him a look and he chuckled to himself.

Jim stood at the end of the aisle and turned around. I could see he had a tear in his eye. Not that he'd ever admit that.

The musicians stopped playing when Mum reached the head of the aisle. Even though I had been dreading this day for ages, I felt calm. Mum and Jim were happy, so why shouldn't I be happy for them? I tried to stop focusing on the wreckage of my life and pay attention to the service. It was fine. The registrar lady was talking about how great marriage is and everyone looked like they were enjoying it. Everything was running smoothly. No weird people shouting out weird things, no dramas, no unexpected interruptions.

Until I heard a noise in the distance.

It started off quiet but grew louder and louder. People in the congregation started to get distracted and the registrar had to speak up.

I surmised it could have been one of two things.

Someone banging two coconut halves together.

Or a horse.

A cold shiver ran through my body.

I leaned back behind Gav to try to see through one of the gaps in the stone. It was no good. The horse seemed to be getting closer. Before I could talk myself out of it, I was out of my chair and tiptoe-running down the aisle. I had a hunch this horse could have been bringing disaster. Gav hissed, 'Where do you think you're going?' at me, but I was away.

I ran past the waiting cars and down the Abbey's drive.

« Older posts

Sure enough, there was a one-horse open buggy coming right at me. I stopped where I was. The driver pulled on the reins and the horse halted.

'Hey, what's the hold-up?' I heard a voice coming from the back. I recognized it.

Dad stood up and looked over. 'Oh, hi, son.'

I folded my arms. It was just as I suspected.

'What do you think you're doing?' I said, trying not to shout but finding it really difficult.

Dad sighed, still standing on the buggy. 'I've been doing a lot of thinking lately, Joe. About our family, your mother, this wedding, and I realized that I still love her.'

'Oh cocking hell.'

I can't take this any more, said Hank. *How do I get out of here?*

'And I love you, son,' Dad went on. 'I want us to be a family again.'

A ball of fury began to burn in my stomach. 'And you wanted to tell her this by gatecrashing her wedding on a cocking horse?'

Dad smiled sadly and scratched his chin. 'It sounds daft when you say it like that, but trust me, it's going to be brilliant. It will take her back to the night I proposed in Central Park.'

The horse huffed and scraped its foot on the floor.

'No,' I said. 'I'm not going to let you do it.'

'What are you talking about, Joe?' said Dad. 'Don't you want us to be a happy family? Come on, move out of the way.'

'No.'

Dad ran his hands down his face. 'Please, son,' he whined. 'I want to show her I'm a changed man!'

I didn't say another word, just turned to the side and lay down on the floor, making it impossible for them to get past without trampling me to death. I was just like that votes-for-women lady.

'Come on, Joe,' Dad cried. 'Let us past, or we'll be too late.'

« Older posts

'That's the idea,' I said.

Dad didn't say anything.

'I'd just like to say that this is super awkward,' said the driver.

I put my hands behind my head and looked at the sky. It was the clearest blue. I couldn't even enjoy that. It just reminded me of Lisa Hall's eyes.

'Fine,' said Dad, his voice all shaky. 'I'll just get out and walk the rest of the way.'

'If you ever want to see me again you won't,' I said.

He didn't say anything.

'What you're attempting is a Grand Gesture,' I said, still staring at the sky. 'And I know for a fact that they don't work. They don't change the way the person feels, they just make you look like an idiot.'

There was silence. In the distance, I could hear the registrar talking.

'But I love your mum, son,' said Dad.

'Mum is happy as she is,' I replied. 'She loves Jim. And if you really loved her, you'd leave her alone and let her be happy . . . Oh.'

It was as if someone had rinsed my brain under the cold tap. Of course. Why didn't I see this all along? Like it or not, Natalie is doing just fine without me. If I truly care about her, I would leave her alone and stop upsetting her. Oh God, I've been a moron all this time. Maybe Troy had a point after all—I did have to look at my dad to figure out how I got to be the way I am.

'I guess you're right, Joe,' said Dad.

'He is, to be fair,' said the driver. The horse huffed again. Even he agreed.

I sat up and looked at the whole ridiculous scene. That is how I will end up if I don't do something.

I mean like my dad. I won't turn into a horse.

I made sure the carriage was out of sight before I re-entered the Abbey. I got there just in time to hear the registrar say, 'I now pronounce you man and wife.' I seized the opportunity of everyone clapping and cheering to slip back into my seat.

'Where've you been, man?' said Gav through gritted teeth.

'I'll tell you later,' I replied, clapping and smiling.

2 a.m.

We headed over to the big function room at Woodlet for the reception. The room was done up so nice that you wouldn't have known it was our crummy school. There

« Older posts

were fancy flowers and the seats were covered in these posh sheet-type things for some reason. It looked super classy.

We sat down and had a 'wedding breakfast', which Gav was disappointed to discover wasn't a full English. Afterwards, there were the speeches. Chips's was mainly him sniggering and saying stuff like, 'Remember that weekend in Blackpool, mate? With the home-made flame thrower? I've been meaning to ask, did your bum hairs ever grow back?'

I could see Harry and Ad sitting at a table with Uncle Johnny, his dummy, Mum's friends Gloria and Glenda, and Jim's workmate Clifton and his wife. I had no idea what they must have been talking about.

After dinner, all the tables were moved and Harry and Ad set up their DJ stuff on the stage. I made sure to stay at the other end of the room, where I was cornered by Great-Aunt Sylvia who shouts for no reason and POKES. YOU. AFTER. EVERY. WORD. WITH. HER. BONY. FINGER.

I could see Harry and Ad trying to catch my eye but I deliberately ignored them. I knew Harry was waiting for the perfect opportunity to give me a cataclysmic bollocking for wrecking their lives.

I kept it up for ages, too—talking to every annoying member of my extended family just to avoid the inevitable confrontation. I had my nose stolen six times, my hair laughed at eight times, and was told I would grow into my looks twelve times. They've been telling me that since I was a baby, but if some of the specimens in my family are anything to go by, it'll never happen.

I was in the middle of a lecture from one of Jim's relatives about how you should never trust the Belgians when I saw someone standing in the doorway. My breath caught in my throat. Natalie. She actually came. I couldn't believe it. She was wearing a bright red dress. It was the first time I had seen her in anything not black. Greeny was with her. They glanced over at me and I quickly averted my gaze.

I excused myself from the foreigner-hating old lady and headed towards the bar. Mum stopped me.

'Hey, son.' She grabbed me in a big hug and spilled some wine down my back.

« Older posts

'Um, hi.'

She let go of me and started picking invisible lint off my jacket.

'You look good, my boy,' she said. 'Very handsome.'

'I think you need to lay off the champagne,' I said. 'It must be affecting your vision.'

Mum lightly tapped my face and laughed.

'Been a strange couple of years, hasn't it?' she said after a while.

I nodded.

'Things have turned out all right though, haven't they?' she said. 'I mean, we're happy, your dad's happy.'

'Hmm yeah,' I mumbled. She will never know how I prevented her wedding from descending into disaster. I'm basically Batman at the end of The Dark Knight. Dad's Harvey Dent. Mum's Gotham.

'I see Nat's here,' said Mum. 'She looks lovely. Colourful.'

I shrugged and looked at the floor. I had been trying to seem happy for the day, but I was already flagging.

'Why don't you talk to her?' Mum squeezed my shoulder. 'She might be more open to being won over at a wedding.'

I gave her a look.

'I'm serious!' she said. 'I mean, I met Jim at a wedding and look where we are now.'

I swallowed the puke explosion in my mouth and forced

a smile. 'I think her mind is made up.'

'Well, you never know,' said Mum. 'Anyway, I've got to carry on making the rounds—we'll talk later.' She stroked my face and kissed me on the cheek. 'Love you.'

A familiar sound drifted out of the speakers. The SOUND EXPERIENCE had been playing Lady Gaga, but this was different. Very different. People came flooding off the dance floor like Black Friday shoppers spotting the last cheap widescreen telly.

'Ugh, what's this rubbish?' Chips whinged. 'It sounds like a bleedin' suicide note set to music!'

I knew what it was: 'Brain Damage' by the Floyd. The greatest song of all time. Without thinking, I squinted through the lights at the DJ booth. Harry was frantically beckoning me.

It seems like they're reaching out, said Norman.

Or it's a trap, said Hank.

I looked towards the bar. I saw Poppy forcing Gav to introduce her to Doris and the Colonel. Gav hadn't looked that awkward since I caught him crying at the first ten minutes of Up.

The music faded down and a voice blared over the PA:

'Joe, get up here, would you, old son? We need to talk.'

Everyone stared at me. I screwed my eyes shut and turned around, heading for the DJ booth as slowly as I could. It was my mum's wedding day. Surely they would go

« Older posts

easy on me. Just tell me I'm dead to them then let me on my way. Standard stuff.

'What's going on?' I said, still unable to look them in the eye.

'Let's go somewhere quiet,' said Harry.

Ad stuck a long megamix on and they led me off the stage and out into the corridor. We kept walking until we reached our old form room. Harry tried the door and found it open. He turned on the lights. It was weird being in there knowing that school no longer held any power over us. It had been the site of so many humiliations—like when I walked in late with my fly open and my SpongeBob pants on show. Or the time I called a teacher 'Mum'. I never heard the end of that. I mean, in a certain light, Mr Fuller did kind of look like her.

I looked around the room—at the sugar paper displays and stacks of textbooks—and it suddenly felt really small and far away, like the scariness had been sucked out of it. Then Ad closed the door behind him and the scariness rushed back. They had taken me away from the party to beat me up—to punish me for my betrayal.

You don't know that, Joe, said Norman. *Don't panic.*

I don't know about that, said Hank. *This has mob hit written all over it. They're going to have him sleeping with the fishes.*

Harry and Ad walked towards me slowly. I'd never seen

them looking so serious before in my life.

'Look, guys, I'm really, really sorry. I didn't mean to blow your big secret—it was an accident. Just don't beat me up.'

Harry and Ad frowned at each other, then burst into laughter. 'Beat you up?' Harry chuckled. 'I should KISS you, you clumsy bum hole.'

The control room didn't know what to do.

'What are you talking about?' I said.

'You blowing our secret is the best thing that has ever happened to us!' he cried, grabbing my shoulders. 'We were the most talked-about thing at *BUZZFEST*.'

'Well, I guessed that,' I said. 'But I thought people would hate you.'

'Not at all, old bean,' said Harry. 'The public has gobbled up Greeny's story. A young man struggling with his identity—secretly in love with the very musical Svengali who had advised the rest of the group to pretend to be gay? It's bloody gold! We have been interviewed for magazines and everything! Look!'

« Older posts

He reached into his jacket pocket and pulled out a piece of paper.

DJ MAG
Who do you guys look up to?

AD
Tall people.

DJ MAG
Ha ha, that's hilarious.

AD
What is?

'Wow,' I said.

'It's been proper good, Joe,' said Ad. 'That bloke who was interviewing me was well cool. He was wearing a retainer even though he didn't need to!'

I chuckled to myself quietly. 'Mila, you're a genius.'

'Seriously, old bean,' said Harry. 'Why do you think we've been trying to call you all week?'

I shrugged, amazed. 'I thought you wanted to tell me to stay away from you forever.'

Harry grinned and shook his head. 'We haven't even told you the best part yet, soldier.'

'Tell him, Harry,' Ad yelped, bouncing up and down like a kangaroo on a pogo stick. 'Go on, tell him.'

'Verity's, Jasmeen's, and Mila's folks' record label are so impressed with our buzz that they want to work with us!' he said.

My heart rate began to normalize. They didn't hate me and weren't going to murder me and dump my body in a landfill! It was a miracle.

'Great,' I said. 'Congratulations.'

'That's not all, Joe,' said Ad, jumping forward and grabbing me by the shoulders. 'They want to work with you, too!'

Him? Hank yelled. *Not even we want to work with him and we're stuck in his brain!*

Norman nodded as if he had a point.

'M-me?' I stammered. 'Why do they want to work with me?'

'Think about it, old son.' Harry paced backwards and forwards, waving his pipe around. 'All our popularity is down to you—the gay gimmick was your idea, getting Greeny on board was your idea, blowing our big secret at *BUZZFEST* was your idea.'

'No it wasn't,' I said.

Harry held up his hand. 'They don't know that. Verity's dad is the vice president of the entire European division and he said he was impressed with your pioneering, risk-taking attitude. He reckons you'll make a top notch A & R man.'

« Older posts

'Um, OK,' I said, all the while thinking, What the hell does A & R stand for? Albert and Rita? The old couple who live over the road? Do they need a man?

'Plus, Mila has been talking you up as an artist,' Harry went on. 'She showed her mum that picture you drew of her and she reckons you have real promise!'

I didn't know what to say. My brain felt like it had removed the saucer section at Warp nine.

'B-but, what about, you know, sixth form? My mum won't be happy if I don't get my A levels.'

'They will work around us,' said Harry. 'We can fit it in around our studies. Our first project is going to be a collaboration with their new rapper, MC Camelface.'

'Oh God,' I moaned.

'Yes, everyone knows that he was your counsellor, too. The press seem to think that this has added a layer of intrigue to the whole story.'

I didn't know what to say. It was all so ridiculous.

'Who else has been invited?' I asked.

'Us three, Greeny, and Natalie,' said Ad. 'Natalie has said no though.'

'Why?'

Ad shrugged. 'Just said she wasn't into the idea.'

'Now are you coming with us or what?' said Harry. 'The girls are going to be here any minute and they're going to want a final answer.'

I looked around the old form room. Yeah, it was horrible but it was familiar. Suddenly the idea of moving into a totally new world seemed terrifying. And deep down, I knew I couldn't leave Natalie. Even though I had given up on the idea of us getting back together, making a leap that huge would be a step too far.

I shook my head. 'No.'

'Are you twanging my dangler, old bean?' Harry said. 'This is a once-in-a-lifetime opportunity you're turning down here. Top industry people are impressed with you. When was the last time anyone was impressed with you? No offence.'

I stared at my old desk. I could still see 'J+N' scratched into the surface.

'Sorry,' I said. 'Can't do it.'

Harry and Ad gave each other a look. 'Promise me you'll give it some thought,' said Harry. 'I know this wasn't ideal—springing it on you at your mum's wedding. It is an emotional day.'

'You're telling me,' said Ad. 'She was supposed to be my bride.'

We headed back to the main room. Mila, Verity, and Jasmeen had arrived and were waiting in the DJ booth.

'Here he is!' Verity yelled. 'Simon Cowley himself.'

'Have you told him about the offer?' Jasmeen asked.

Harry nodded. 'He is considering it. Svengalis like Joe don't like to rush into things.' He winked at me and slapped me on the back.

'I hope you say yes, Joe,' said Mila.

I stopped and looked at her. My stomach turned over.

'I'm amazed that you ever want to see me again, to be honest.'

She laughed. She looked really different away from *BUZZFEST*. Her hair was pinned up in an emerald comb and her Floyd tattoo peeked out over the top of a strapless green dress.

'Hey, we've all done stupid stuff after a broken heart,' she said. 'Believe me. When my smeerlap ex back in Amsterdam finished with me, I climbed into his bedroom on a ladder and emptied a bucket of fish over his imported hair products.'

'Wow.' I laughed. 'I didn't know you were so angry.'

Mila took a sip of her drink and swished the ice around her glass. 'That was a big turning point for me,' she said. 'I realized that no boy is worth getting that upset over. Since then, I have become a much calmer person.'

'Just as well,' I said. 'Because with the way I acted at *BUZZFEST*, I should be due a ton of rancid fish. I'm, uh, sorry about that, by the way.'

Mila leaned across and touched my cheek. Without wanting to, my whole face flared bright red. 'It's fine,' she said. 'Now you go and do your wedding thing—I'll see you when you come and work for PGS.'

I nodded and caught Natalie's eye on the other side of the room. She held my gaze for a couple of seconds before looking away.

There was no way I could go. I'm no Svengali. Everything I've done for the *SOUND EXPERIENCE* has either been spur-of-the-moment stupid or an accident. I'd be there five minutes before they figured me out. No, I'll stay in Tammerstone, mess up my A levels and get a job at McDonalds. If I apply myself, I could earn a star by the time I'm thirty.

I jumped off the stage and bustled through the dance floor. Auntie Sylvia broke away mid-'Macarena' and planted a wet, slobbery, lipsticky kiss on my cheek before I could escape. I was just wiping my face with my pocket hanky when I felt a hand on my shoulder. Who this time? Did Chips want to rub my scalp until I was completely bald?

I turned around.

'Ah—oh, Greeny. Hi.'

Greeny beamed at me. I'd never seen him smile like that. When he smiled before, it was like he was holding back, like he couldn't let himself be properly happy. This time it was different. His whole face lit up.

« <u>Older posts</u>

I went to speak, but he held his hand up. 'I know you feel bad about what happened, but you shouldn't.'

'Wha?' I said.

'I gave you a hard time for years because I hated myself so much,' he said. 'If anything, I should apologize to you. I'm sorry, Joe.'

I didn't know what to say. 'Um . . . that's OK?'

'I keep thinking back to that night at the Easter prom,' he went on. 'When I had it out with you over there by the crisps. I was so close to telling you how I felt, but then at the last second, I got scared. I couldn't do it. I kept telling myself that it was a phase—that one day I would wake up and start fancying girls. It wasn't until I told Natalie that I could admit it to myself. But even then, I didn't want anyone else to know. I still felt ashamed. Stupid, isn't it? But when you accidentally told everyone Harry and Ad were straight, I saw my opportunity to finally let the world know who I really am, and I've never been happier. I mean, tomorrow night I have a date with a boy! Can you believe it?'

I smiled. 'I'm very happy for you, Greeny.'

'Thank you,' he replied. 'And I'm looking forward to working with you at the record label.'

I glanced over at Natalie again. I wasn't sure how long she had been watching us. 'I don't think I'm going,' I said.

Greeny's big smile faded. 'Well, whatever you decide, I wish you the best,' he said. And then he did something weird. OK, maybe not weird, but it was weird to me. He kissed me. Seriously. Full on the lips for about three seconds.

My word, said Norman.

I . . . I don't know how I feel about this, said Hank.

Afterwards, he gave me a wink and walked away smiling to himself. I looked around and saw loads of guests staring at me. Great-Auntie Teresa crossed herself and said a Hail Mary. Mum smiled at me and mouthed, 'It's OK.'

Unbelievable. I hurried out of the room as quickly as I could with my head down and didn't stop until I was outside. And I don't know whether it was Harry or Ad who played me out with 'YMCA' but whoever it was it was totally not funny.

I turned right out of the door and climbed up the bank to the field. The sun had just set and the sky was a deep blue. I sat down on the bench and closed my eyes. It had been such a weird day and my brain felt like a bag of angry ferrets. There was so much to think about, I didn't know where to begin. When did life get so complicated? It only seems like yesterday that I was eight years old, playing in the woods with Harry and Ad, daring them to run up to the Goatman's house and touch the door. Mum and Dad were still together, I was just getting into **STAR TREK** and it didn't even occur to me that girls were any more interesting than boys. I miss it in a way.

The fading strains of 'YMCA' drifted out of the hall. It

« Older posts

sounded strangely relaxing from far away—kind of like whale song or a babbling brook. I could feel myself drifting off. At least sleep would take me away from real life, if only temporarily. I breathed deeply and tried to quieten my chattering brain.

'Sleeping on benches now? God, things have got rough for you, haven't they?'

My eyes shot open and I looked to the left. There was Natalie, sitting next to me. An electric charge swept through my body from my feet to the top of my bristly scalp.

'Um . . . hi,' I said.

She smiled. 'Hi.'

I looked out at the field. Mad Morris had wandered in at some point and was giving a sermon about John the Baptist to a flock of pigeons.

'I saw your moment with Greeny just then,' she said. 'Just thought I'd come and check it hasn't awakened anything in you.'

I laughed. It was weird in a way. I'd been fixated on her for so long that I forgot how funny she was.

'I feel like I'm saying this a lot today,' I said. 'But I'm sorry. I really am.'

Natalie sighed. 'Look, Joe. For the last time, I'm not taking you back, OK?'

I rubbed my eyes. 'I know,' I said. 'But that's not why I'm saying it. I'm saying it because I mean it.

You're a brilliant person and you didn't deserve what I put you through. I've realized a lot of things about myself today.'

She didn't say anything. It felt good to say that. To forget all those stupid Grand Gestures and what was basically borderline stalking. If I'd have done that to begin with who knows what might have happened?

'I would have forgiven you, you know,' said Natalie, out of nowhere.

'Wow, are you actually a mind reader?' I said.

Natalie laughed and smoothed her dress against her legs. 'Yeah, why not?'

'What did you mean by that though?' I asked.

'If you'd kissed anyone else,' she said. 'Literally anyone but Lisa.'

'Why's that?'

Natalie pushed her fringe out of her eyes. 'Because it was people like her that made my life hell. Made me feel ashamed to be different. When I met you, it was like discovering another world. A world where people liked me for who

I was. Where I could be myself and not have to worry about being ridiculed. When I saw you kissing her, that world was destroyed. It just reinforced everything I already knew: I'm not good enough.'

I'm not sure when I started crying, but by the time she finished talking, I was in full flow. I was so upset, I couldn't even feel embarrassed about it.

Natalie scooched closer to me and dried my cheeks with her thumbs. 'But I don't want you to feel bad any more, OK?' she said. 'It's over. Done.'

I tried to take a deep breath but my lungs were like the engine in Jim's knackered old van.

'You have to move on with your life,' she said. 'Everybody else is: Harry and Ad have been signed by a record label, Greeny is working with them as well as studying at college, I'm doing my A levels and have a job I really love. You're the only one who's stuck in the past.'

I didn't know what to say. I knew she was right.

'Please tell me you're going with Harry and Ad,' she said.

I shrugged. 'Wasn't planning to.'

She whacked me on the shoulder. 'Why the cocking hell not?'

I made a 'don't know' noise.

'It's because of me, isn't it?' she said. 'You don't want to leave me behind?'

I shook my head, then nodded. Natalie put her arm

around my shoulder. That old buzzing feeling that I used to get when we held hands came back, but this time it was different. It was more pain than excitement.

'Do it,' she said. 'Even if you hate it and quit after a week, at least you'll have tried.'

I still couldn't speak.

'You have to move on,' she said again. 'All this obsessing about me isn't healthy, OK? And as much as I hate to say it, I'm not that great.'

My sobbing shifted up a gear. 'You are though,' I said. 'You're the best thing that ever happened to me.'

She rubbed my shoulder and gently shushed me. I shook my head and carried on anyway.

'It's just—it's just I love you and I can't get around the fact that you don't love me any more.'

Natalie moved her hands to the sides of my face, pulled me close and kissed me. It was just like our first kiss at the Easter prom, sitting on the same bench. But while that felt like the beginning of something, this . . . this didn't.

Natalie broke off the kiss and ran her hands over my bald head. 'I'll never stop loving you, Joe Cowley,' she said. 'I wish I could.'

She let go of me and stood up. 'I'll see you around, yeah?' she said.

I nodded, too stunned to speak, and watched her walk away.

I headed back into the room after a while. It was dark and Mad Morris had spotted me. By the time I got back, Harry and Ad were playing a slow song and the dance floor was full of couples drunkenly swaying to the music. I didn't especially want to sit at a table on my own so I went up on stage, only to find that Harry and Ad were slow dancing with Verity and Jasmeen. Mila leaned against the wall on her own. She glanced up at me and smiled.

What Natalie said whirled around my brain. She was dead right. While everyone else was doing something with their lives, I was trying to move backwards and reclaim the past. I looked out at the dance floor. Mum and Jim gazed into each other's eyes as they danced. Gav had given in and was full-on snogging Poppy up against a pillar. Doris laughed as the Colonel slowly twirled her around. Even the dummy in Uncle Johnny's arms looked quite content.

Soon, Natalie was going to college and Harry and Ad would be off to London all the time to work on *SOUND EXPERIENCE* stuff. Where would that leave me? All alone in my room, being miserable and listening to babies cry.

Before I could talk myself out of it, I pushed myself away from the speaker stack and tapped Harry on the shoulder. He looked up at me, kind of irritated, as I think he was about to go in for a snog with Verity.

'I've had a rethink,' I said. 'I'm going to come with you.'

Harry was so excited he nearly shoved Verity to the ground.

'Did you hear that, old bean?' he yelled at Ad. 'Joe's coming!'

Ad laughed. 'Wicked.'

'No, not like that, you ignoramus,' said Harry. 'He's going to be our manager again!'

Ad, Verity, and Jasmeen cheered and exchanged high fives.

'That is awesome, Joe,' said Jasmeen. 'I promise you won't regret it.'

I smiled as best I could, but I still wasn't sure. I walked away and leaned against the wall. I honestly didn't know if I could just start again. Natalie had been my reason to live for ages—firstly as my girlfriend, and then as this kind of distant, unreachable figure that I couldn't get out of my mind. What was I going to do without her?

« Older posts

I pulled out my phone and scrolled through my drawings—it starts off with the ones of me and Natalie, all hearts and unicorns. Then it gets darker—the graves, the crows, the lonely old man in a nursing home. Then I came to the last one.

My sketch of Mila on that burger tray seemed to jump out from the screen. I hadn't looked at it since *BUZZFEST* so I was shocked by how different it was to what came before. Almost like a new chapter. Behind her is a huge crowd and a stage with a band playing, but what draws you in are her eyes and her smile.

I felt a warm hand wrap around mine. I followed it up the arm and to the real smiling face of Mila.

'Hi,' she said.

'Hi,' I replied.

Mila squeezed my hand. 'Everything is going to be all right, you know,' she said.

I looked at Mum, then Gav, then at Harry and Ad, then back at Mila. For the first time in nine months, the gloomy fog lifted from my brain.

'Yeah,' I said. 'Maybe it is.'

And that was when Boocock ran in.

The End

Or is it . . .

To be continued . . .

JOE COWLEY

returns in

Straight Outta Nerdsville

Spring 2017

BEN DAVIS

Since he was a little boy, people told Ben Davis he would grow up to be an author. He didn't listen at the time, because he thought he was going to be an astronaut or play up front for Man United. When he reached his mid-twenties without a call from NASA/Fergie, he realized that maybe they had a point and started writing again. First, Ben wrote jokes for everything from radio shows to greeting cards. Then, he moved on to stories. He chose to write for young adults, largely because his sense of humour stopped maturing at the age of fifteen. Ben lives in Tamworth with his wife, son, and dog.

Find out more about Ben at the
Not So Private Blog of Ben Davis:
bendavisauthor.blogspot.co.uk

You can also visit his website:
bendavisauthor.com

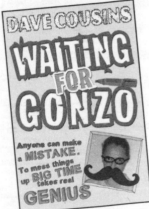

More fantastic
books
I reckon you'll like.